"I may not remember what I've done, but I don't think I'm the only one with secrets."

Grace's heartbeat quickened. "What do you mean?"

Ethan gazed down at her. "I don't know who you are any more than I know who I am. We're strangers...and yet, we seem to have some kind of connection. Even you can't deny that."

"Our connection is my sister," Grace tried to say calmly.

He shook his head. "I don't think so. I can't help but wonder if you're holding something back from me. Did we know each other before?"

"No." Grace's heart pounded. He was getting too close. If he found out who she was...

"Then what is this connection we have?" he asked almost urgently.

Grace shrugged. "Attraction. Chemistry. Call it what you like."

"Why do I feel as if it's something more?" Ethan grabbed her arms and pulled her to him. "Why do I know how your lips would taste if I kissed you right now? How your body would feel beneath mine if we—"

"Please don't," Grace said breathlessly.

He drew her close, so close their lips were only a heartbeat apart. "You want me to kiss you," he murmured against her mouth. "Tell me to stop...."

Dear Reader,

You've told us that you love amnesia stories—and in response we've created a program just for these incredibly romantic, emotional reads. A MEMORY AWAY—from danger, from passion... from love!

This month, award-winning author Amanda Stevens brings you her ninth Intrigue, *Lover, Stranger,* a deeply passionate story about a man with no memory and the woman who loves him against all odds. Amanda makes her home in Cypress, Texas, where she lives with her husband of twenty-three years and their twelve-year-old twins.

We hope you enjoy this and all the special amnesia books in the A MEMORY AWAY program.

Sincerely,

Debra Matteucci
Senior Editor & Editorial Coordinator
Harlequin Books
300 East 42nd Street
New York, NY 10017

Lover, Stranger
Amanda Stevens

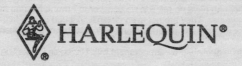

TORONTO • NEW YORK • LONDON
AMSTERDAM • PARIS • SYDNEY • HAMBURG
STOCKHOLM • ATHENS • TOKYO • MILAN • MADRID
PRAGUE • WARSAW • BUDAPEST • AUCKLAND

ISBN 0-373-22511-3

LOVER, STRANGER

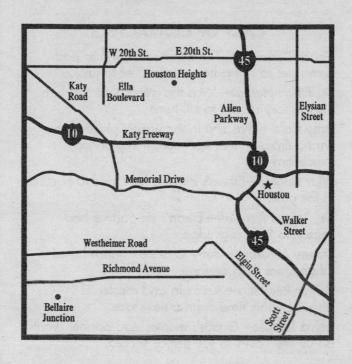

CAST OF CHARACTERS

Grace Donovan—The bitter secret in her past drove her to bring her sister's killer to justice.

Dr. Ethan Hunter—Was the attack that cost him his memory meant to kill him?

Amy Cole—Was she in the wrong place at the wrong time, or was her murder a planned execution?

Pilar Hunter—Ethan's ex-wife had tried to hurt him in the past.

Dr. Robert Kendall—Ethan's ex-partner had reason to hold a grudge.

Danny Medford—Amy Cole's ex-fiancé hated Ethan more than anyone.

Trevor Reardon—Assassin and master of disguise—this time, with a new face.

Myra Temple—Grace's mentor and partner would do all she could to see justice served.

Chapter One

His lungs were bursting as he thrashed his way through the jungle, trying to elude his predators. Over the lacy treetops, the moon rose full and majestic, illuminating the path of broken limbs and trampled grass he left in his wake. It was only a matter of time before they picked up his trail.

The sky was clear and inky black, like a giant, obsidian bowl that had been turned upside down and painted with thousands of tiny, white stars. Pausing to catch his breath, he searched for the brightest star among them, Polaris, the north star that would guide him toward the village. There he would hopefully find a phone, or at least transportation to take him out of this godforsaken place. If he could somehow make it to the border...

Off to the west, he heard the rumble of an engine, distant at first, but drawing steadily near. A beam of light from a high-powered searchlight arced over the terrain just missing him, and then moments later, he heard shouts. Laughter. His trail had been discovered. The killers were closing in, and they were enjoying the hunt.

Heart pounding, he plunged through the lush foliage.

Low-hanging branches slapped at his face and arms while man-sized roots tangled with his feet. Amber eyes, ruby eyes, emerald eyes glowed from the trees and from the darkness all around him. Every step was a new danger, a new terror. God, how he hated the jungle!

Finally stumbling into a clearing, he found himself on the edge of a jagged precipice. Mist rose from the raging river that sliced its way through the limestone cliffs a hundred feet below him. Ahead, the ravine sprawled into a yawning gap of nothingness. Behind him, the shouts of his pursuers rose in excitement as they spotted him in the moonlight.

There was nothing to do but head back into the jungle for cover. But before he could run, gunfire echoed through the stone canyon. The noise was so muted by the mist, the scene so surreal, that for a moment, he hovered at the edge of the precipice, unsure what to do. Then he felt the sharp blast of pain in his side, looked down and saw the blood and realized he'd been hit. Realized he wasn't going to make it to the village, much less to the border.

As if in slow motion, he fell backward into nothing but vapor and air...

"DR. HUNTER? Can you hear me?"

He opened his eyes and saw a woman's face leaning over him. Dressed all in white, she looked radiant. Other-worldly. An angel, he thought. So he hadn't made it after all.

"Dr. Hunter?"

He blinked as the angel spoke again. Was she talking to him? She was gazing down into his eyes, smiling, but that name she kept calling—who was Dr. Hunter?

"He's coming around, Dr. Kendall," she said over her shoulder.

A man appeared beside her. He wore the same look of concern on his face as she did, but he wasn't smiling and his eyes were dark with something that might have been suspicion.

"Well, well," he said. "Glad to see you've decided to rejoin the land of the living, Ethan. You certainly gave us all a scare tonight."

Ethan? Who was Ethan?

He closed his eyes for a moment, trying to clear his head. Obviously he was in a hospital somewhere. These people seemed to know him, but he'd never seen them before in his life. Nor had he ever heard of anyone named Ethan Hunter. It had to be a case of mistaken identity, but—

A tiny bubble of panic floated to the surface of his consciousness. If he wasn't Ethan Hunter, who the hell was he?

He searched his mind and found no answers.

"How are you feeling, buddy?" Dr. Kendall peered down into his face.

Buddy? Did that mean the two of them were friends?

But Kendall didn't look particularly friendly. In spite of his easy bedside manner, there was something about his eyes, a glimmer of hostility that was faintly unnerving.

The man they called Ethan stared up at him, frowning. "I feel sort of…out of it." The sound of his own voice shocked him. It was raspy and coarse, and the effort to speak hurt his throat. He put a hand to his neck and winced at the pain. The skin was bruised and tender.

Dr. Kendall must have glimpsed the fear in Ethan's

eyes for he said, "Take it easy. Your vocal cords and larynx have been stressed. Don't try to talk any more than is necessary."

Ethan tried to swallow past the pain and the panic. "What happened?"

"We're hoping you can tell us."

He thought for a moment. "I had this strange dream about running through a jungle... Someone was trying to kill me."

Kendall's shrug was dismissive. "I'm not surprised. You've sustained a concussion. You look like hell, but you're damned lucky to be alive."

You look like hell...

The realization hit him suddenly that he had no idea what he looked like. He put his hands to his face. The skin was bruised there as well, and a thick bandage wrapped around his skull.

Scanning his surroundings, he searched for a mirror but didn't see one. Which was probably just as well. If the pain in his face was any indication, he wasn't at all sure he was ready to see his reflection.

"What were you doing at the clinic tonight, anyway?" Kendall asked suddenly, his tone edgy.

"I'm...not sure." Ethan squeezed his eyes closed, trying to remember what had happened to him, but nothing came to him. He tried to fight back the suffocating panic that threatened to engulf him. *Who the hell am I?*

Stay calm, a little voice warned him. *You have to figure this thing out. Your life could depend on it.*

He drew a long breath. Okay. He just needed a few minutes to get his bearings. There was no cause for alarm. He had a concussion. Short-term memory loss was common enough with head injuries, wasn't it? Maybe they could even give him something—

But wait a minute. If he was a doctor—Dr. Ethan Hunter—he would know that, wouldn't he? He would know how to treat a concussion and temporary amnesia. He would know how to cure himself.

But he didn't. He didn't know anything at the moment, and his panic came rushing back.

Dr. Kendall touched his arm, and Ethan flinched. Why didn't he like this man? And more importantly, why didn't he trust him enough to confess his amnesia to him?

As if reading his thoughts, Dr. Kendall's eyes narrowed. "The police are outside, Ethan. We've stalled them as long as we can, but there's a detective who's been champing at the bit ever since you were brought in. Are you up to talking with him?"

About what? Ethan wanted to know. But he remained silent. For some reason he didn't understand, it seemed imperative that he not give himself away. That he remain calm and as much in control as he could be under the circumstances.

But just what the hell *were* the circumstances? Why couldn't he remember who he was?

The door of his hospital room opened, and a man wearing an ugly green suit walked in. He was in his early fifties, stoop-shouldered, with salt-and-pepper hair slicked straight back and plastered with hair cream. His face was deeply creviced, his eyes shadowed with years of hard service and even harder drinking.

He walked over to Ethan's bed, pulled up a stool and sat down. Removing a yellow number-two pencil and a black notebook from his inside jacket pocket, he licked the lead of the pencil, then scribbled a hasty note. Without looking up he said, "So you're Dr. Hunter."

Ethan said nothing.

"I'm Sergeant Pope, HPD."

HPD. Ethan searched his mind. Honolulu Police Department? Harrisburg? Hartford? Houston? Where was he?

Wait. There was an unmistakable twang in the detective's easy drawl. Okay, so they were probably in Houston, but why? Did he live here?

He glanced up, and as his gaze met Pope's for the first time, Ethan sensed a keen intuition and intellect that belied the faint air of ennui that settled like an old blanket over the aging detective.

Watch yourself, Ethan thought, though why he should fear the police he had no idea. Was it because in his dream, the Mexican authorities had been chasing him through the jungle? Was that why an almost innate sense of wariness had surfaced the moment the detective had walked into the room?

"I've heard a lot about you," Pope was saying. "My wife showed me an article about you in the paper a couple of months ago. Had a real nice shot of you in your downtown office, but I can't say you look much like that now."

Ethan thought about the thick bandage wrapping his skull, the raw bruises on his face and neck. "No, I guess not."

Pope thumped the pencil eraser against his notebook. The sound was barely audible, but for some reason it grated on Ethan's nerves. "The article told all about that free clinic you built in the Mexican jungle, and how you spend several weeks a year down there, operating on underprivileged kids. They gave you quite a write-up. The wife was real impressed." The thumping stopped suddenly. "Hey, I'll have to tell her I met you tonight."

"Sure, why not?" Ethan said, because he didn't know what else to say. His throat still hurt. He reached for the glass of water on the stand beside his bed. The nurse—Nurse Angel, he now thought of her—was instantly at his side, helping him to drink. Her hand wrapped around his on the glass. Her touch was soft, caressing. Intimate.

When Ethan lay back against the pillows, he saw that Pope was watching him. The detective had seen the encounter. Ethan was sure of it.

Pope said, "She was thinking about calling you. My wife, that is." He put a finger to his nose and pressed it to one side. "She has a deviated septum like you wouldn't believe. She's been wanting a nose job for years."

So...he was a plastic surgeon? Somehow Ethan would never have guessed that.

Almost inadvertently his gaze dropped to his hands, resting on top of the sheet. There was dried blood caked beneath his nails and a wedding band on the third finger of his left hand.

His heart raced when he saw the ring. If he was married, where was his wife? Had she been contacted? Shouldn't she be at his bedside at a time like this?

As if on cue, Nurse Angel moved back into his line of vision and gave him a knowing wink.

Pope, momentarily distracted by the nurse's dazzling smile, said, "Listen, will y'all excuse us? I'd like to speak to Dr. Hunter alone."

Dr. Kendall nodded tightly, then turned to Ethan. "Dr. Mancetti said she'd be back tonight to check on you. In the meantime, if you need anything, I'll be around for a while."

"Great," Ethan said, though he didn't have the faintest idea who Dr. Mancetti was, nor did he have any intention of calling on Dr. Kendall's services.

Nurse Angel bent over Ethan's bed, fluffing his pillow and patting his arm. "I'm pulling a double shift tonight," she confided in a throaty whisper. "If you need anything, Dr. Hunter, *anything at all,* you just call me."

"Thanks," he murmured, his gaze lingering on the sway of her hips beneath her snug uniform as she turned and walked out of the room.

Sergeant Pope seemed mesmerized by the movement, too. For a moment, neither man spoke, then the detective mentally shook himself. "The staff here seem pretty concerned about your welfare, doctor. You must be a popular guy." There was a mocking glint in his eyes as his gaze dropped to the wedding ring on Ethan's finger.

Ethan resisted the urge to hide his hands, caked blood and all, beneath the sheet.

For a moment, Pope busied himself with his notes. Then, his voice edged with a weariness Ethan didn't trust, he said, "We may as well get this over with. I'd like to file my report and get home before midnight, and you look like you could do with some rest." He paused. "Can you tell me what happened tonight?"

Ethan shrugged. "I'm afraid the details are still a little sketchy." He made a vague gesture toward his head. "The concussion…"

Pope nodded. "I spoke with your doctor a little while ago. She said it might be a few hours, or even a few days before you could fill in all the blanks. But let's just go over what you do know."

Which is nothing, Ethan thought. *Nada.*

The only thing he could remember was the dream. Running through the jungle. Being pursued by men who wanted to kill him. And falling...falling...

Then, like a bolt of lightning, another memory shot through him. He was in a room that contained an examination table, metal cabinets and a sink. He felt groggy, out of it, but he could smell antiseptic. Knew, dimly, that he was in a place he didn't want to be.

Someone was in the room with him. Someone with a gun...

"I remember being in a doctor's office," he said, almost to himself. "In an examination room, I think."

"You were found at your clinic here in town," Pope supplied.

Ethan put a hand to his head, touching the bandage. "Someone was with me. A man. I think we fought. I heard a woman scream...then gunfire...then..." He trailed off as his head exploded in pain. He clutched his temples with his hands. "I was hit with something hard...something metal..."

"We think it was a flashlight," Pope said. "We found one with blood on it at the crime scene, but we won't know if it's your DNA until we get it back from the lab."

Ethan closed his eyes, trying to remember the rest, but his recollection was hazy at best. In some ways, the jungle dream was much clearer to him. But was it more than a dream? Was the jungle scene somehow connected to what had happened to him earlier in that office?

Why couldn't he remember? Why didn't he know who he was?

He groaned, whether from actual pain or memory, he wasn't sure.

"Did you recognize the man in your office?" Pope asked.

It had been dark inside the examination room, but the blind at the window was open and moonlight flooded in. The man was wearing a ski mask, but Ethan could tell that he was staring down at him in the pale light, grinning as he aimed the gun at Ethan's face. "Got to make this look good, pretty boy," the gunman said, as he turned to the drug cabinet behind him and rifled through the medication, choosing and discarding with an expertise that was chilling.

By contrast, Ethan's movements were slow and lethargic. Almost dreamlike. It was as if he were caught in an invisible web he couldn't break free of.

Then, unexpectedly, the door to the examination room opened and a woman screamed. As the gunman whirled toward the sound, Ethan, acting on pure instinct and adrenaline, lunged toward him. The gun went off as Ethan crashed into the man, dragging him downward. From the doorway, where the woman had screamed, the only sound was a thud, a soft moan, then silence.

The gun came free as the man hit the floor. Both he and Ethan scrambled toward it, but the weapon slid out of reach beneath a steel cabinet. As the two of them fought, Ethan became aware of a siren in the distance. Someone had heard the gunshot and called the police. The man must have heard the siren, too, for his struggles became even more desperate. More deadly. He got his hands around Ethan's throat and squeezed, squeezed, until stars exploded inside Ethan's head.

From somewhere deep inside Ethan, a primal urge, some killing instinct rose to the surface, and he reached upward, his thumbs finding the man's eyes. The man screamed and released him, but before Ethan could use his advantage, the gunman found a new weapon. He grabbed something metal from the floor and struck Ethan's head a vicious blow.

Dazed, Ethan fell back. Before he could regain his strength, his equilibrium, the man was on him. He hit Ethan's head...his face...again and again until blackness mercifully swallowed the pain.

Ethan glanced at Detective Pope. "That's all I remember." But at least now he knew how he'd gotten the bruises and the concussion, how his vocal cords had gotten stressed. What he didn't know was why. "I don't know what happened to the gunman after I lost consciousness, or why he didn't kill me."

Pope's gaze flickered over Ethan. "My guess is, he panicked. He heard the sirens and ran. Not likely we'll find any prints on the flashlight or anywhere else. I suspect he went to that clinic prepared. He knew exactly what he was looking for."

"Which was?"

"Drugs, more than likely."

Ethan touched a bruise on his cheek, remembering the blows, wondering if his face resembled a slab of raw meat, because that was the way it felt.

Got to make this look good, pretty boy.

He hadn't related that part of the memory to Sergeant Pope. Nor did Ethan say what he was now certain of—that the gunman hadn't gone to the clinic looking for drugs. He'd gone there to kill Ethan.

Then why not tell the police? that voice inside him demanded.

Because his instincts told him not to. Because Ethan was very much afraid when the truth came out, when he finally remembered everything, there might be a chance a cop would be the last person he could turn to for help.

He realized Pope was watching him again, and Ethan tried to shutter his expression, tried to hide his fear and dread.

"Can the rest of this wait until morning?" he asked suddenly, wanting to be rid of the detective. Ethan knew instinctively that he had to watch his step as he had never had to watch it before. Someone wanted to kill him. It was like a drumbeat inside his head. Someone wanted to kill him, and he had no idea who. He didn't even know who he could trust. For all he knew, Sergeant Pope was the enemy.

Was it Ethan's imagination, or had the detective's expression suddenly turned suspicious?

"I'll try to make it quick. Just a few more questions," Pope said, paging backward in his notes. "Let's see…oh, yeah, here we are." He paused, reading, then glanced up. "Dr. Kendall told me you'd been in Mexico for the last couple of months or so. He said you were due back three weeks ago, but you'd had some emergency surgery down there. An appendectomy, I think he said. You weren't supposed to travel for several more days, but then you decided to come back tonight. Why the sudden change of plans?"

The jungle dream came rushing back to Ethan. He could smell the dank scent of rotting vegetation, could see the Hummer's lights bouncing over the uneven terrain, could actually feel the throb in his side from the bullet.

Or was the pain from the appendectomy incision? Was the dream nothing more than a drug-induced vision while he'd been under the knife?

He said vaguely, "I had something I needed to take care of."

One of Pope's brows rose in surprise. "Must have been pretty important if you were willing to risk your health."

Ethan hesitated, not knowing how to respond. *You're a doctor, so think like one. Why would you come back from the jungle before you were supposed to?*

Aside from the fact that the Mexican authorities were trying to kill you....

But Ethan didn't think he wanted Pope to know that. So he said instead, "There's a patient I have to see."

"Is that why you went by the office tonight before going home?"

"How did you know I didn't go home first?"

"Your luggage was still at the clinic. So was your wallet and briefcase. We'll get everything back to you as soon as we're finished with it."

"Thanks," Ethan mumbled, his mind racing. A wallet would contain a driver's license, credit card, money. A home address.

Sergeant Pope said, "From your story, I gather the gunman was already inside the clinic when you arrived."

"I'm pretty sure he was," Ethan said, though he wasn't at all sure of anything. His first memory was of staring up into the gunman's masked face. Ethan had no recollection of getting off a plane, arriving at the office, or of anything else.

Except fleeing through the jungle…

He remembered that all too clearly.

"Did you call your assistant and ask her to meet you at the clinic?" Pope asked.

"My assistant?"

"The woman who walked in on you and the gunman. Amy Cole."

Dammit, be careful. "Oh, yes. Amy." Ethan wondered if he'd answered a little too quickly because Pope's gaze narrowed on him. "How is she, sergeant? She wasn't seriously hurt, was she? She saved my life tonight."

Something flickered in the detective's eyes. "Dr. Kendall didn't tell you?"

"Tell me what?"

"Amy Cole's dead. Shot right through the heart. Poor kid never knew what hit her." Pope shook his head. "Damn shame, a beautiful woman like that."

Ethan felt the air leave his lungs in a painful rush. He had no recollection of the woman, didn't even remember what she'd looked like, but he could still hear her scream. Could still see, in his mind's eye, the gunman whirl toward the door and fire.

And now Ethan was more certain than ever that the gunman had come to the clinic to kill him. Amy Cole, whoever she was, had taken a bullet that was meant for him.

Whoever *he* was…

Chapter Two

"This is suicide, Dr. Hunter. I won't allow you to do it." A middle-aged, stoutly built commando in a nurse's uniform planted her hands on her hips and blocked Ethan from the door to his room. The lines in her weathered face were deeply etched and as unyielding as the starch in her pristine uniform.

Ethan had hoped to slip out of his room unnoticed and make his exit before anyone missed him, but this woman—he glanced at her name plate—Roberta Bloodworth had caught him in the act. What a name for a nurse!

"Don't worry," he lied as he finished buttoning his blood-stained shirt. "I'm feeling much better. All I need is a good night's sleep in my own bed."

Actually, he felt like hell. His head throbbed, his face hurt, his whole body ached as if he'd been hit by a bulldozer. But the pain was the least of his worries. At the moment, he didn't even know where his own bed was, or who he should be sharing it with.

All he knew was that he had to get out of here. He had to find some answers. Somehow he had to figure out who was trying to kill him, and why.

"Just look at you," the nurse scolded. "I hardly

even recognize you, and the way you sound, like some horror movie ghoul." She wagged her finger in his face. "And I shouldn't have to remind you how dangerous a head injury can be. You shouldn't be alone tonight."

"I won't be alone." He slipped on his suit jacket. "My wife will take care of me."

"Your…wife?"

Too late, Ethan realized his mistake. He'd made assumptions about the ring on his finger that obviously he shouldn't have made. Were he and his wife separated? Divorced?

Damn. Was he widowed?

He gave her a wink. "Well, let's just say, I won't be alone, okay?"

"Same old Dr. Hunter," she grumbled, but there was a spice of mischief in her close-set eyes as she continued to challenge him.

Ethan sensed that beneath her gruff exterior, she held a genuine affection for him. It made him feel a little better. Maybe everyone wasn't his enemy after all.

But…could he trust her enough to tell her about the amnesia? Would she be able to help him?

Or would she insist on calling the police? Or worse, Dr. Kendall?

Ethan still couldn't shake the notion that Kendall held a deep malice toward him. What had happened between them in the past?

For a moment, he considered asking the nurse about Kendall, but something warned him not to. Something told him not to press his luck with Roberta Bloodworth because she, of all people, might see right through him.

He tried to smile disarmingly. "Anyway, you know what they say about doctors. We make the worst patients. You should consider yourself lucky to be rid of me."

She threw up her hands in exasperation. "All right, it's your funeral. Why should I care?" But as she turned toward the door, he heard her murmur, "Take care, Ethan."

After she left, Ethan checked the pockets of his jacket. A stick of gum, a parking stub, a Post-it note with a phone number he didn't recognize. As if they were precious gemstones, he carefully returned the items to his pocket. Opening the door, he quickly surveyed the corridor, then stepped out, searching for the nearest exit. He spotted the elevators and headed toward them as the bell pinged on one of the cars and the door slid open.

A woman emerged, looking windblown and slightly breathless. Their shoulders touched as they brushed by each other, and for a moment, their gazes locked.

Ethan's immediate impression was that, for the most part, the woman's features were neither beautiful nor plain, but fell somewhere in the category of interesting. Her eyes, however, were extraordinary, so light a blue they almost appeared translucent.

She wore a tailored navy pant suit, and her dark red hair was cut short and tucked behind her ears, in a style that was deceptively simple. She looked professional, no-nonsense, a woman with a definite purpose.

All this Ethan saw in a heartbeat, a man noticing and acknowledging an attractive woman. With a mumbled, "Excuse me," he entered the elevator, giving her hardly more than a second thought. But just before the doors slid closed between them, he saw her turn and stare after him, in a manner that filled him with unease.

Did he know her?

He started to press the open button to confront her, but what would he say? How could he be sure she was a friend and not an enemy? Maybe she'd come to the hospital to finish the job someone else had botched earlier.

Not a pleasant thought, but one he couldn't ignore. Truth was, he couldn't afford to trust anyone.

As he left the elevator and headed through the hospital lobby toward the street entrance, he tried to take stock of what he had learned about himself. His name was Ethan Hunter. He was a plastic surgeon. He was married...or at least, had been married. He had just returned from Mexico, where he'd undergone an emergency appendectomy, and he'd been badly beaten tonight by a man who had wanted to kill him.

The wound in his side tingled as he pushed open the glass door and stepped outside. A blast of hot air greeted him, and he realized it must be summer in Houston. Even though it was late, after ten, the cloying heat was almost suffocating.

He could see the city's impressive skyline in the distance and wavered for a moment, unsure what to do, where to go. Maybe it hadn't been such a great idea to leave the hospital. He should have at least figured out where he was going first. Maybe he should have somehow gotten his wife's number and called her to come and get him.

Somehow that didn't seem to be an option he wanted to explore. Neither was waiting around in a hospital room for his would-be killer to come and find him.

Ethan couldn't explain it, but he hadn't had a choice in leaving the hospital. He'd been compelled to flee. He knew he had to run. Knew he couldn't afford to stay in one spot too long.

Headlights arced across his face, and he threw up a hand to shield his eyes. For a moment, he thought he was back in the jungle. He could see the searchlights scouring the mountainside. Hear the rush of water below him. Feel the sharp punch of the bullet as it entered his side. Then he was falling…falling…

Someone grabbed his arm, and Ethan whirled, reaching blindly for his enemy, pulling the body tightly against him as he pressed his arm into a soft, pliant throat.

GRACE DONOVAN SAW her entire life flash before her eyes. The arm that pressed against her windpipe was like an iron vise. The more she struggled, the harder he squeezed. Forcing herself to go limp, she waited for the infinitesimal relaxation of her assailant's muscles, then she chopped upward, using both hands as she'd been taught.

His hold loosened without breaking, but at least she could breathe. She gulped air into her lungs, then stumbled away when he finally released her.

"Are you crazy?" she managed to gasp.

He was looking at her as if she were a ghost. He stared at his hands, then back at her. Then stared at his hands again. "I could have killed you." His skin looked deathly white in the sodium-vapor streetlight.

"No sh—kidding." Grace massaged her throat, glaring at him. Headlights swept across his face, causing the bruises to stand out starkly against his pallor. "Why did you attack me like that?"

He was still staring at his hands. "I don't know."

Grace kept her own hand at her throat, suddenly feeling very vulnerable and not liking it. "Look, you don't have to worry," she said dryly. "I don't think there's any permanent damage."

He glanced up, his brown eyes shadowed with an emotion Grace couldn't define. "You're okay then?"

She frowned. "I'll be fine, but I wasn't talking about myself. I meant you…your hands. You're a surgeon, right?"

He didn't answer, just stood staring at her in the gloom. Grace shivered even though it was June and the heat rising from the concrete was thick enough to cut with a scalpel. She could feel her hair curl at the back of her neck, but wasn't sure whether it was because of the humidity or the man standing before her…the way he was looking at her.

She cleared her throat. "You are Dr. Hunter, aren't you? Dr. Ethan Hunter?"

"Do I know you?"

He took a step toward her, and Grace fought the urge to retreat. It wasn't like her to be so easily spooked, but the bruises and bandage gave him an almost maniacal look as he stared down at her. There was something about his eyes…a darkness that was chilling. She wondered, fleetingly, what she was getting herself into.

"We've never met. But I saw you briefly upstairs."

"At the elevator," he said, as if it had just occurred to him.

She nodded. "I came here to see you. The nurse told me you'd checked yourself out. Do you think that's a good idea? If you don't mind my saying so, you don't look so good."

"I'm fine." As Grace watched, he lifted his fingertips to probe his battered face. The action reminded her of a blind man, trying to "see" with his hands.

''Why were you looking for me?'' he asked suddenly.

She released a long breath, not realizing until that moment she'd been holding it. ''I want to talk to you about what happened tonight. I've spoken with the police. They told me about the shooting. I've just come from the morgue.''

She had his full attention now. His brown gaze scoured her face. ''The morgue?''

Grace wrapped her arms around her middle, shivering suddenly as if she were still in the cold-holding room where Amy's body had been taken. This was the important part. It was crucial that she convince him. ''I want to talk to you about Amy Cole.''

Something flashed in his eyes. Regret? Guilt? Or was it merely a trick of the light? ''You knew Amy?''

''She was my sister.''

He looked stunned. ''I'm sorry. I don't know what else to say.'' He spread his hands in supplication, glancing away, then back at Grace. ''She saved my life tonight.''

Despite the hoarseness, his voice was deeply compelling. Dusky and sensual, it called forth emotions from inside Grace she had no wish to unveil. Not now. Not when so much was at stake. Not when her sister's death was on the brink of being avenged. Nothing else could be allowed to matter. Certainly not a man with a battered face and a voice as seductive and deadly as a storm-swept sea.

She tried to conjure up an image of her sister, but the memories had faded.

Ethan touched her arm, and Grace jumped as if she'd been burned. ''Are you all right?'' he asked.

She swallowed over the sudden fear in her throat.

"I'm fine. But unfortunately, my sister isn't. That's what I want to talk to you about. I want to know why Amy's dead, Dr. Hunter. I want to know what you had to do with it."

The shadows in his eyes deepened. "What do you mean?"

"I think you know exactly what I mean." Grace forced herself to remember the past. To use her emotions. She unfolded her arms, letting one hand grip her purse strap. The other hand balled into a fist at her side. "I know all about you and Amy. Your *affair*." She all but spat the word at him and saw him wince as if she had physically struck him.

When he didn't try to defend himself, Grace said coldly, "She told me all about it. She also told me that you'd gotten her involved in something dangerous. Something she said might end up getting you both killed, and it looks like she was right."

This time, he didn't flinch at her words. He stared at her with eyes as cold and dark as a moonless winter night. "I don't know what you're talking about."

"Oh, I think you do." She lifted her chin. "Amy's dead, Dr. Hunter, and I think you know more about her murder than you're saying. I came here to get some answers, and I'm not leaving without them."

"Then you may be waiting a long damn time." He turned to walk away from her, then stopped suddenly, looking around at the street and passing cars.

Grace walked over to him and caught his arm. The muscles beneath her hand flexed defensively, like tempered steel. Her hand dropped to her side. "You can't just walk away from this. You owe me the truth. You owe it to Amy. She was in love with you, dammit!"

His fingertips brushed against the bandage. He suddenly looked very lost. "I didn't know."

Grace glared at him, telling herself not to react to his emotions, to the look of desperation lurking in the depths of his eyes. He was a dangerous man, and she couldn't afford to forget it.

"What do you mean, you didn't know? Amy never told you how she felt? You must have guessed. She was never very good at hiding her feelings."

He glanced down at Grace, as if on the verge of confession. Then he shrugged and turned away. "I'm sorry about your sister. Deeply sorry. But I can't help you. There's nothing I can tell you. I don't have the answers you're looking for."

"Then you leave me no choice." Grace opened her purse and took out a stack of envelopes tied with a blue ribbon. "Amy wrote to me regularly in the past few months. These are her letters. They're all about you, Dr. Hunter. About the promises you made to her. The favors you asked of her. I'm sure the police would be interested in seeing them."

He turned at that, his expression stark in the streetlight. Whatever flash of vulnerability Grace might have glimpsed earlier had vanished. His gaze narrowed on her. "Is that threat supposed to frighten me? Why should I assume the police would have any interest in your sister's letters? What did she accuse me of?"

Grace hesitated, meeting his gaze. Then she glanced away. "All right, I admit, she never mentioned anything specific. But she said enough to arouse my suspicions, and I think her letters might make the police more than a little curious as well."

"Then why haven't you already handed them over?"

"Because I wanted to talk to you first."

"Why?"

"I have my reasons."

He studied her for a moment. "Is it because you're afraid your sister may not be an innocent bystander in..." he made a vague gesture with his hand. "...all this? Is it because if you go to the police, they may start to probe a little too deeply?"

His perception surprised Grace. "That's part of it," she admitted reluctantly. "But it's more than that. I don't exactly trust the police."

That seemed to interest him. He lifted a dark brow. "Why not?"

"Because Amy is just a statistic to them. Another case. One of a dozen homicides that take place in this city every week." She paused, biting her lip. "But she was my sister, Dr. Hunter, and I'll do anything to bring her killer to justice. Right now, you're the only one who can help me do that."

His brow rose again, but when he remained silent, Grace pressed her point. "I don't want to go to the police, but if that's the only way I can gain your co-operation—"

He moved swiftly, grasping her forearms and hauling her toward him. Grace started to struggle away, but something in his eyes, a terrible look of desperation, made her momentarily yielding.

"Don't you understand?" He gazed down at her, his eyes darker than Grace could ever have imagined. "I *can't* help you. I don't know anything."

"Then why are you so afraid of the police?" she asked, unable to tear her gaze from his. Her breath caught in her throat. She wondered, suddenly, if she had pushed him too far.

For a moment, he seemed to undergo some intense inner struggle. A myriad of emotions flickered across his features, then he let his hands drop from her arms and backed away from her. "I don't know anything about your sister. About those letters. About our…relationship. I don't remember her. I don't even remember my own name or what I look like. I don't remember anything. Is that clear enough for you?"

Grace stared at him in shock, watching the shadows flicker across his features. Where he stood, one side of his face was in light, the other in darkness. It was a strange illusion, almost as if she were talking to two distinctly different men. Unnerved, she said, "Are you telling me you have amnesia?"

He didn't answer, just stood there staring down at her. He was dressed in a suit, dark gray and beautifully tailored. The jacket was open, and Grace could see the dark droplets of blood on the front of his white shirt.

That, more than anything, reminded her of why she was here. Her heart jolted uncomfortably. "My God," she said. "You don't remember *anything?*"

"Not much," he muttered. His expression became shuttered again, as if he were already regretting his confession.

But had it really been a confession? Was he telling her the truth, or trying to cover his tracks?

Damn, Grace thought. *Amnesia could change everything.*

She tried to assess this new situation while wondering if she should proceed as planned. She stared at him for a long moment, watching for the telltale flicker of desperation she'd glimpsed earlier, searching for a flash of fear, anything, that might give him away.

But she saw nothing. It was as if a mask had descended over his features. In some ways, this masquerade of control frightened her more than anything else, because it showed her how easily he could deceive her if he chose to.

"What did the doctor say about your condition?" she finally asked.

He shrugged. "I understand it may take days, or even weeks, to fill in the blanks."

"From what you just said, it sounds like we're talking about more than a few blanks."

He shrugged again.

Grace glanced around, realizing how vulnerable they were standing out in the open. In spite of the intense heat, she shivered. "Look, maybe it isn't such a great idea for you to be on the street like this."

"I'm fine," he said, almost angrily. "Don't worry about me."

"You're not fine," she countered. "You were almost killed tonight. Hasn't it occurred to you that whoever did this to you...to Amy...could come back?"

"That's not your problem." But she knew he had thought of it. She could see it in his eyes. She wondered if that's why he'd left the hospital.

"Well, I'm sorry, but I've made it my problem," she said, backing her shoulders. Staring him down. "I want to find my sister's killer, and at the moment, you're my only clue. I'm not letting you out of my sight."

He scanned the night sky, as if looking for guidance. Searching for the way home. His expression looked bleak in the moonlight. "What was it you said earlier? Amy told you I'd gotten her involved in something dangerous? Something that might end up getting us both killed? Wasn't that it?" His gaze met Grace's and she shuddered. "If I were you, I wouldn't want to be standing between me and the next bullet."

SHE FOLDED HER arms over her breasts, in a manner that was unmistakably determined. He saw that same stubbornness in the set of her jaw and chin. In the way her gaze met his without wavering. "I told you. I'm not going anywhere until I get some answers."

"And I told you, I don't have those answers."

"Yes, you do. You just don't remember them. That is, if you really do have amnesia."

"You don't believe me?"

Her blue eyes flickered, but she said nothing.

Ethan told himself her opinion of him didn't matter, but for some reason, anger shot through him. She didn't even know him. She was basing her judgment solely on what she'd heard from her sister. And if he and Amy Cole had been having an affair…if the relationship had gone bad…

The wedding ring on his finger was suddenly a dead weight. He resisted the urge to remove it. For all he knew, he might still be deeply in love with his wife…ex-wife?…estranged wife?

Then why would he have had an affair with Amy Cole?

Ethan shook his head, trying to clear the fog, but the haze only deepened. So many things he didn't know. Couldn't remember. What had happened to him in Mexico? What had he been involved in that had gotten Amy killed tonight?

He stared down at her sister. His initial impression of her remained. She was a woman with a definite purpose, but there was something in her eyes that belied her tough exterior. The pain of her sister's murder?

Guilt stabbed through him. Amy Cole may have died because of him. He wouldn't be responsible for another woman's death. "Look," he said. "I don't care whether you believe me or not. I'm getting the hell out of here. And if you're smart, you won't follow me."

She took a warning step toward him. "You're not getting away from me that easily."

"Don't be stupid," he said in exasperation. "I don't want you to end up like your sister."

Something flashed in her eyes. A momentary look of uncertainty. "I won't. I'm not Amy. I can take care of myself."

He shook his head in regret. "You don't know what you're getting yourself into. *I* don't even know."

"I know that I won't rest until I find my sister's killer," she said softly. Her eyes glowed with an emotion so deep, so fierce that Ethan felt unsettled just watching her. "Can you really afford to send me away? Where will you go? Do you even know where you live? At least let me get you off the street. Let me take you someplace where you'll be safe."

He stared at her for a long moment, trying to resist the temptation she placed before him. "I don't want to get you involved in this."

"Don't be stupid," she said, flinging his words back at him. "What choice do you have?"

"Actually, there is choice," he said slowly. "I could still decide to go to the police for help."

She gave him a sidelong glance. "I don't think so."

Meaning he *couldn't* go to the police. Meaning whatever he had been involved in was not something he would want the cops to know about.

Like it or not, she had him exactly where she wanted him.

"All right," he said. "I guess we're stuck with each other. For the time being, at least."

Her expression was anything but triumphant. "Looks that way. Come on. My car's over here."

As Ethan followed her to the parking lot, he had a feeling that he was walking blindly into something every bit as dangerous, every bit as deadly as the jungle.

Chapter Three

They headed west on Memorial Drive. Ethan knew this because he studied the road signs, hoping to recall a memory. Though they were in the middle of the city, the street became progressively more wooded. The streetlights along the dark green colonnade illuminated high walls and gated drives. Ethan glimpsed large houses beyond the walls, with curving driveways and lush vegetation skillfully showcased by landscaping lights that gave everything a soft, green glow.

Ethan searched for something familiar, a landmark that would strike a chord, but the street remained as unfamiliar to him as his own name. As his own face.

He touched the bruises and grimaced. It was time to evaluate the damage. "Do you have a mirror in here?"

She threw him a surprised glance. "On the visor, but—"

"What?"

"Be prepared," was all she said.

He pulled down the visor and slid back the cover on the lighted mirror. It was so narrow, he could only see a portion of his face at a time. He adjusted the visor, staring first at the thick bandage on his forehead, then at his eyes—both of which were blackened and one almost completely swollen shut—then at the ugly, raw bruises on his cheeks, and finally his lips, cut and also swollen. Kendall had been right. He looked like hell.

He looked like a stranger.

Adjusting the mirror again, Ethan returned to his eyes. Dark brown, what he could see of them. Black lashes. Thick eyebrows. He ripped the bandage from his head and heard her gasp.

"You probably shouldn't have done that," she muttered.

Black hair, matted with blood, tumbled over his forehead, covering the long crescent of stitches over his left brow.

Got to make this look good, pretty boy.

Ethan didn't say anything for a long moment. Couldn't say anything.

She braked for a light, and he could feel her watching him. But he couldn't tear his gaze away from his reflection.

"It's all superficial," she said softly. "The cuts and bruises are only skin deep. They'll heal. In a few days, you'll look like a new man."

He studied his eyes, searching for the windows to his soul. A new man? What had the old one been like? A doctor who operated on poor children in Mexico? A husband who cheated on his wife? A man who had gotten a woman killed tonight?

He could still feel her watching him, and he turned suddenly, capturing her gaze. She looked momentarily startled, as if she'd just seen him for the very first time. Or as if she'd glimpsed something in his battered features she hadn't expected.

Was there a redeeming quality hidden among that mass of bruised flesh?

He wanted to think so. He fervently wanted to believe it.

"You're a very good-looking man," she said suddenly.

He almost laughed. "In a Frankenstein sort of way."

"No, I'm serious." She glanced in the rearview mirror. Then glanced again. The light changed, and the car accelerated. "Trust me, you're very handsome."

"I thought you said we'd never met."

He saw a brief frown flicker across her features. "We haven't, but I've seen pictures of you. Amy showed me."

Amy. He tried to conjure an image of the dead woman, a memory of his feelings for her, but he felt nothing. Saw nothing.

He studied the woman beside him. Her profile was shadowed in the subdued light from the dash, and she kept glancing in the rearview mirror, as if she expected them to be followed. He wished he knew what she was thinking, and why he couldn't bring himself to fully trust her.

There was something about her...

Something about the pain in her eyes...

He had no doubt that she'd experienced grief. That her sister's death had affected her deeply, but the pain seemed muted somehow, not sharp and fresh as one would expect. Amy had only been dead a few hours.

This woman seemed too in control. Too determined.

Her gaze left the road for a moment to meet his. He felt an odd stirring somewhere inside him. Suspicion? Desire? Funny how those two emotions weren't mutually exclusive of each other. Far from it.

"Do you look like her?" he asked.

She turned back to the road. "You mean Amy? Not

really. She was fair like me, but blonde. And she didn't have freckles. She was thinner than me. Taller. Very beautiful.''

Was that a trace of envy in her voice? Ethan said, ''I don't even know your name, or where you're taking me. I don't even know why I should trust you.''

''Which question should I answer first?''

He paused. ''The last one, I guess, because depending on your answer, the other two might not matter anyway.''

Her blue gaze touched his again. Again he felt the jolt. ''Have you ever heard the expression Honor Among Thieves? That sort of fits us, I guess. You can't go to the police without possibly incriminating yourself, and for reasons of my own, I don't want to involve the authorities, either. The only way you can protect yourself is to find Amy's killer before he finds you. And as it happens, that's the same thing I want. It makes sense that we help each other.''

''Even if we don't exactly trust one another?''

She shrugged. Ethan thought her answer couldn't have been more eloquent.

After a moment, he said, ''And if we do find Amy's killer. What happens then?''

She didn't hesitate. ''I bring him to justice. After that, I don't give a damn what happens to you.''

''That's cold.''

''It's honest.''

She braked for another light, but this time, she didn't look at him. She stared straight ahead, her hands gripping the steering wheel.

''So,'' she said, ''do you still want to know the answers to the first two questions?''

He almost smiled. ''Surprisingly enough, yes.''

She did glance at him then. Her eyes seemed like starlight. Soft and clear. Very mysterious. "My name is Grace Donovan. And I'm taking you home."

He lifted a brow, felt the faint pulling at his stitches. "Your home?"

"No, yours."

The light changed and the car started forward.

"How do you know where I live?"

"Amy showed me once."

He paused. "Has it occurred to you that we may not be able to get in? I don't have keys."

"Did you check your pockets?"

"Of course. The police have my wallet and brief-case, along with whatever luggage I brought back from Mexico."

"Let's hope they don't find anything incriminating," she said. "At least not until we see it first."

She was blunt to the point of brutal. Ethan had to admire her guts. "What makes you think my house will be safe?"

"Wait till you see the place. It's like a fortress."

Ethan tried to picture his home. Tried to imagine himself living in a house that could be described as a fortress, but the only thing he could conjure was the smell of the jungle, the roar of the river, the adrenaline rush of danger. Somehow those things seemed more familiar to him than the estatelike homes they were passing on Memorial.

After a moment, he said, "Your last name is Donovan, not Cole. Are you married?"

"Actually, no. Amy was, briefly. Right out of high school. It lasted about a year. The guy was pretty much a lowlife. She always did have lousy taste in men." Their gazes clashed—hers defiant, his oddly defensive.

He said, "Can I ask you something? You say you want to find your sister's killer, but—"

"But what?" she asked sharply.

"You don't seem exactly...torn up about her death."

He saw her knuckles whiten on the steering wheel. "Because I'm not crying? Not falling apart? Because I want to see her killer brought to justice? There are different ways of expressing grief, Dr. Hunter. Believe me, I know."

"I'm sure that's true. But you seem so—" Again he floundered for the right words, and she turned to stare at him in challenge. "In control," he finally said.

"I don't consider that a bad thing. Do you?"

"Amy's only been dead a few hours."

"No one's more aware of that than I am." She shot a glance in the rearview mirror.

"What about your parents? Have you called them?"

"Everyone's been notified who needs to be," she said. "You don't need to concern yourself with my family. Or with my emotions, for that matter."

"But I feel responsible for Amy's death, even if I didn't pull the trigger. I need to know about her," he said urgently. "I need to know what kind of person she was. Why she became involved with me—other than the fact that she had lousy taste in men."

"I'm sorry. That was a cheap shot," she allowed almost grudgingly. "Look, I may as well tell you. Amy and I weren't very close. In fact, until a few weeks ago, we hadn't spoken in years."

Surprised, he studied her profile in the dash lights. "Why?"

She shrugged. "We had a falling out. It was stupid,

but we just never made up. Resentment and jealousy have a tendency to run a little too deeply, you know?''

He heard the pain and regret in her voice and said instinctively, ''Was it over a man?''

She grimaced. ''How very perceptive of you. That man she married right out of high school? He was my fiancé.''

Ethan didn't know what to say to that. In the silence, she laughed, a brittle little sound that didn't quite ring true. ''Guess I have lousy taste in men, too.'' She paused again, drawing a breath. ''Maybe now you understand why my emotions may not be what you think they should be. But I am grieving for my sister, in my own way. And I'll have to live with all these regrets. That's why it's so important for me to find Amy's killer. To focus on getting her justice. Because if I don't…if I let this guilt eat away at me…'' Her eyes closed briefly. Her hands trembled on the steering wheel. ''This is the last thing I can do for her, Dr. Hunter. Do you understand?''

''I think so.'' Ethan was more affected by her words than he wanted to admit. He turned to stare out the window.

Beside him, Grace murmured, ''She was only twenty-four. Just a baby. Did you know that?''

The scenery blurred past Ethan. ''Do you know how old I am?''

''Thirty-seven, according to Amy.''

''Am I still married?''

When Grace didn't answer right away, he turned to stare at her. She shrugged. ''As far as I know, a divorce was never anything but a promise.''

''Then my wife—''

She shrugged again. "May be at home waiting for you. We'll soon find out."

She turned into a long, circular drive, coming to stop in front of a house that could only be described the way she had earlier—as a fortress. Nestled in a forest of ancient oaks trees and towering pines, the house was white and bleak, a modern, four-story structure with walled courtyards, security cameras and a windowless bottom floor.

The wall of glass blocks on the second floor reflected soft light from within, as if someone were indeed home waiting for him. Ethan stared up at the stark lines of the house and wondered what he might find inside. His past? A wronged wife?

Neither prospect buoyed him.

"How do you propose we get in?" he asked doubtfully. "I already told you, I don't have keys, and even if I did, I wouldn't be able to turn off the alarm system."

"Why don't we just go ring the bell?" Before he could protest, Grace got out of the car and strode toward the courtyard gate.

Dread hanging like a dark cloak over his shoulders, Ethan opened the door and followed her.

When he stood next to her, Grace pressed the button on the intercom, and after a few moments, a voice sputtered over the speaker. "Yes?"

Grace opened her hands, palms up, as if to say, "You're on," and Ethan cleared his throat. "It's me. Ethan. I forgot my key."

A surprised silence ensued, then a woman with a Spanish accent said, "Dr. Hunter? I'm so glad you're finally home. *Un momento, por favor.*"

Almost immediately the lock on the gate was disengaged from inside the house, and the gate swung open. They walked through the lush courtyard toward the front door. Somewhere on the grounds, Ethan heard a sprinkler, and a dog barked in the distance. He glanced up at the winking light on the security camera mounted inside the gate, and thought again of the jungle. Of eyes watching him in the darkness.

The door was drawn back, and a tiny woman wearing a gray-and-white uniform appeared in the light. She took one look at Ethan and gasped, her hand flying to her mouth.

"Dr. Hunter, are you all right?"

"I will be," he assured her.

"Dios Mío." Quickly she crossed herself, then took his arm, murmuring in Spanish while she gently ushered him inside. "What happened?"

"It's a long story."

As she fussed over him, Ethan tried to study his surroundings without giving himself away, but it was hard to contain his reaction. The inside of the house was even more overwhelming than the outside. The jungle theme of the courtyard had been carried through to the foyer, and—he discovered moments later when they climbed a circular staircase—to the second-floor living room.

Giant palms and tree ferns stretched toward a vast ceiling of skylights, while dozens of potted orchids with magnificent purple, yellow and white blooms added to the exotic atmosphere. From his perch across the room, a huge blue-and-yellow parrot tracked them with beady, knowing eyes.

It was like being back in that jungle. Ethan suddenly felt claustrophobic. He allowed the maid to lead him to a deep leather chair, and wearily he sank into it.

She drew up an ottoman for his feet, still muttering and clucking like a mother hen. "What happened, Dr. Hunter?" she asked again when she finally had him settled to her satisfaction. "Was there an *accidente?*"

"He was mugged," Grace said.

The maid whirled, as if she'd only now discovered Grace's presence. She turned back to Ethan, her dark eyes wide and frightened. "Should I call the *policía?*"

Her English was almost flawless when she chose it to be. Ethan had the impression her lapses into Spanish were more by design, a reminder, to herself perhaps, of the heritage she'd long ago left behind.

"I've already spoken with the police," he told her.

She wrung her hands. "I knew something was wrong. I expected you home hours ago. When you called from the airport in *Méjico,* you said your flight was on time. Then you didn't come…" She broke off, her gaze easing back to Grace.

Ethan said, "This is Grace Donovan. She gave me a ride home from the hospital."

Grace walked over beside Ethan, and the maid's gaze followed her, narrowing.

"How do you do?" Grace held out her hand. The maid took it tentatively. Grace said, "I'm sorry. I don't believe I caught your name."

"Rosa."

Nicely done, Ethan thought, although why he felt the need to hide his amnesia from his housekeeper he had no idea. He hadn't told Dr. Kendall or Sergeant Pope of his memory loss, either. He hadn't confided in anyone but Grace, and again, he didn't know why, except that she was Amy's sister, and he'd felt he owed her something. Some sort of explanation.

She was only twenty-four years old. A baby.

He fingered the bruises on his throat, in some perverse way welcoming the pain.

Rosa said anxiously, "Can I get you something? *¿Agua? Té?*"

"No, thank you." For the first time, Ethan noticed a shopping bag and purse on the white leather sofa beside the chair where he sat. He glanced at Rosa. "Were you on your way out?"

She looked faintly uncomfortable. "*Sí.* I was going to stay with my daughter tonight. She has a new *bebé*, remember? Her husband is out of town, and tomorrow is my day off. We talked about this on the phone earlier, but with everything that's happened—" She broke off, staring down at him, shaking her head. "*Tu linda cara...tu pobre linda cara...*"

Ethan automatically put a hand to his face. "Don't worry. It looks a lot worse than it is. You go on. Go be with your daughter. I'm fine."

She looked doubtful, but Grace said, "Yes, don't worry about Dr. Hunter, Rosa. I'll look after him."

Rosa's gaze darkened disapprovingly. "What about Señora Hunter?"

"What about her?" Ethan asked, tensing.

Rosa hesitated. "She called earlier. She said Dr. Kendall told her you were coming back tonight. If she comes here and finds you—" Her gaze shot to Grace. "Last time...the acid...your car..."

Ethan exchanged a glance with Grace. To Rosa, he said, "Look, don't worry. I can handle Señora Hunter. You go be with your daughter and *nieto*. I insist."

She glanced at Grace, shaking her head and muttering, "Trouble," as she turned and collected her purse and shopping bag from the sofa. "*Mucho* trouble."

GRACE WANDERED AROUND the magnificent living room while Ethan followed Rosa downstairs. She could hear them murmuring in low tones, but couldn't tell what they were saying. After a few moments, their voices faded, and Grace assumed they'd walked to the back of the house, where a rear entrance probably led to the garage.

After a few minutes, Ethan came back into the room from a different entrance, and Grace turned to him expectantly. "Everything okay?"

He nodded. "I told Rosa the concussion was playing tricks with my short-term memory. I asked her to help me with the alarm code."

"Did she?"

"Everything's set. We're armed and dangerous."

"I like the sound of that," Grace murmured. She felt the weight of her gun in her purse and almost smiled. Thank goodness it hadn't been necessary to use force to convince him to cooperate with her. Not yet at least.

"Did you get that part about your wife? 'The acid…your car.' I wonder what happened."

Ethan's mouth thinned. "I'm not sure I want to know. Sounds like we have a real loving relationship."

Grace sensed that Rosa's words bothered him more than he let on. She said reluctantly, "Do you think she found out about your affair with Amy? Maybe it was a sort of *Fatal Attraction* in reverse."

He turned away. "I really don't want to speculate on the state of my marriage."

"But we have to," Grace said. "That's the only way we'll find answers."

He turned to stare at her. "Do you really think my wife had something to do with Amy's murder?"

Grace shrugged. "It wouldn't be the first time jealousy got out of hand."

His gaze, if possible, darkened. "Is that what Amy intimated in her letters? Was she afraid of my wife?"

"She mentioned her a few times. She called her Pilar. I think there'd been some trouble. But I think the danger Amy referred to came from a different source. Something to do with your clinic in Mexico. If you're up to it, I thought we might go over her letters together. Something might jog your memory."

He ran a weary hand through his hair and walked away.

"Of course, we don't have to do it right now," Grace murmured.

He didn't seem to hear her. He wandered around the room, touching a table here, a chair there, as if he could somehow absorb the essence of the room, of who he had been, into his consciousness.

After a few moments, the almost preternatural silence got to Grace. She walked over to stand beside him. "This is quite a place."

He traced the curved stem of some exotic potted flower, then clipped a red bloom with his thumb nail, as if the delicate blossoms were no more rare or precious than a dandelion. The scarlet petals fell like drops of blood to the surface of the glass table. "It feels more like a prison than a home," he finally said.

"A prison?" Grace glanced around the spacious room. The dense foliage gave the illusion of nature at her most primal, and the enormous skylights afforded a magnificent view of the night sky. She made a sweeping gesture with her arm. "It seems more like a jungle to me. Wild. Primitive. Look, you can even see the moon."

Ethan glanced up, and Grace could have sworn she saw him shudder. He turned away, heading toward a door at one end of the long room. He opened it and switched on a light.

Grace came up behind him. "What's in there?"

"Looks like an office or a study."

"That should be a good place to start searching for clues, right?"

She sensed him tense. He seemed reluctant to enter the room.

Grace said, "Want me to go first?"

"No," he said over his shoulder. "I'll just have a quick look for now."

Grace frowned. Obviously he didn't want her following him into the study, but why? What was she afraid she might find?

She turned and walked back to the middle of the room. A movement to her right startled her, and she whirled, automatically grabbing for the gun in her purse. But then she saw the huge parrot preening himself, and realized she'd forgotten all about him. He'd been quiet and still since they arrived, but now all of a sudden, he'd grown restless.

Grace tentatively approached his perch. His movements weren't restricted in any way. She supposed he could fly around the room if he chose to, but all he did was take a couple of nervous, sideways steps on the perch.

A cage with an open door sat on a pedestal near the perch, and Grace guessed that was where he took his meals and got his water. Maybe he was even trained to go potty there as well, she thought, because the room was immaculate.

She stood a couple of feet back from the perch and

watched him for a moment. His beady little gaze held hers. "Hey," she said softly, trying not to alarm him. "What's your name?"

He cocked his head and continued to stare at her.

"What's the matter?" Grace asked. "Cat got your tongue?"

All of a sudden, he let out a piercing squawk and flapped his wings so vigorously that Grace screeched, too, and covered her head. When he made no move to attack, she let out a breath of relief and relaxed.

"Sorry," she told him. "It was just a figure of speech." She could have sworn the bird looked sullen and put out. Grace decided she'd better make peace. Moving toward him, she made a kissing sound with her lips and crooned, "Polly want a cracker?"

"Look at the size of those headlights!" the parrot screeched.

Grace jumped at the unexpectedness of his speech. At the crudeness of his words. She gaped at him in shock. "What did you say?"

The bird repeated the line.

"That's what I thought you said."

The parrot fluffed his wings. "I don't think they're real," he said importantly.

"How would you know, you little buzzard!"

Grace's tone seemed to excite him. He raced sideways along the perch, squawking in a loud voice, "They're not real! They're not real! I should know, goddammit!"

"Why you—" Grace made a menacing move toward the parrot, but he put up such a fuss, she instantly retreated.

Behind her, Ethan said, "What's going on? I thought I heard voices."

Grace quickly took several more steps away from the bird. "Your little friend here and I were just having a rap session."

"That thing can talk?" Ethan walked toward the parrot.

"I wouldn't get too close," Grace warned. "He's a little…unpredictable."

But the enormous bird was on his best behavior for Ethan. They stared at each other for a long moment, then Ethan said, "What's your name, fella?"

"What's your name, fella?" the bird said in perfect imitation.

Ethan laughed, a sound that sent a shiver sliding up Grace's spine. "All right, I'll go first. My name's Ethan. At least…I think it is."

The parrot blinked. "My name's Ethan," he mimicked.

Ethan glanced at Grace. "This is getting us nowhere fast. You try."

Grace shook her head. "I don't think so. I don't care for birds." Not this particular bird, anyway.

Ethan turned back to the parrot. "Her name's Grace."

"Look at the size of those headlights!"

Startled, Ethan jumped, then his gaze flew to Grace. A spark of amusement—or was that curiosity?—flared in his brown eyes, and Grace's face flamed as his gaze dropped almost imperceptibly to her chest.

He turned back to the parrot. "What else can you say?"

"I don't think they're real." The bird looked straight at Grace. Then he strutted and preened on his perch.

"Proud of yourself, aren't you?" she muttered. She

pointed at Ethan. "How about picking on him for a change?"

As if he understood her every word, the bird cocked his head and stared at Ethan. "Hey, pretty boy."

Grace threw up her hands. "That does it—" She broke off when she saw the look on Ethan's face. He had grown very still, his expression grim as he turned away from the parrot.

"What is it? Did you remember something?"

Behind them, the parrot gave a long, shrill wolf whistle. "Hey, pretty boy. Hey, pretty boy," he sang.

Ethan flinched. "No, it's not that." His gaze didn't quite meet hers. "I'm just tired. I think I'd like to get some rest now."

Grace got his meaning loud and clear. He wanted her to leave. He wasn't about to invite her to spend the night here.

But she was reluctant to let him out of her sight. He'd sustained a concussion, among other injuries, and probably shouldn't be alone. And, contrary to what he'd said, she was almost certain the parrot had triggered a memory for him. Why wouldn't he admit it? Why wouldn't he tell her?

"I'm a little worried about you," she said. "I don't think it's a good idea for you to be alone tonight."

He shrugged. "You said yourself, this place is like a fortress. Now that I know how to arm the alarm system, I should be safe enough."

Grace bit her lip. "Maybe. But I'm not just talking about that. You've got some pretty serious injuries. A head trauma. That's nothing to take lightly."

He looked at her then, his expression ironic. "You don't have to worry about me. I'm a doctor, remember?"

His words did nothing to reassure her. But there was very little Grace could do, short of forcing him at gunpoint to let her stay. She fingered her purse strap, considering.

"If you're sure…"

"We can talk more tomorrow." His tone was final.

"Well…I guess I'll see you in the morning then," Grace said reluctantly.

They started down the stairs together, and he put his hand on her elbow to guide her. Grace was surprised that she didn't pull away, and even more surprised that she didn't *want* to pull away. The touch of his hand sent a shiver of awareness down her backbone. It should have frightened her, but instead, it reminded her that she was still alive. Still a woman. And it had been a very long time—too damned long—since any man had done that for her.

They paused in the foyer while Ethan turned off the alarm system. Then he opened the door, and pressing another series of buttons, disengaged the lock on the courtyard gate. He followed her outside, and they stood in the driveway to say their goodbyes.

It was nearing midnight. The air had finally cooled, and a lazy breeze drifted through the ancient trees, sounding like rain. The moon was still up, almost full. The freshly watered lawn glistened like diamonds in the milky light, and on a trellis outside the courtyard, a moon flower opened to her lunar mistress.

The night was beautiful, clear and starry, but Grace knew the darkness could be deceptive. She peered into Ethan's eyes, wondering what secrets were hidden deep within those fathomless depths.

Moonlight softened his bruised and battered face, and for a split second, Grace had a glimpse of what he really looked like. She caught her breath, remembering what she'd told him earlier. He was a good-looking man, but she thought his allure had little to do with his physical appearance, and everything to do with the man beneath. The mysteries he had unwittingly buried.

She had the sudden and unexpected urge to kiss him, to see if it would stir his emotions enough to uncover those secrets.

As if sensing her scrutiny, he turned and captured her gaze. Grace wondered fleetingly if he could tell what she was thinking. If he knew what she wanted at that moment.

She was almost certain that he did.

"I'd better be going," she murmured, realizing too late just how dangerous her situation had suddenly become.

But when she would have walked away, he caught her arm, turning her back to face him. Their gazes met again, his deep and mystical; hers, she feared, open and far too revealing.

"Thank you for bringing me home tonight," he said. His voice, deep and raspy, had an unnerving affect on Grace.

"You don't have to thank me," she said. "I had my own reasons for doing so."

"Still—" He broke off, his gaze moving away from her. "I'm sorry about Amy. I hope you believe that."

At the mention of Amy, an image of Grace's sister came rushing back to her, reminding her of exactly why she was here. What she had to do.

"If you really mean that," she said softly, almost regretfully, "then I shouldn't have to convince you to help me find her killer."

"I don't think we'll have to find him," Ethan said,

his gaze suddenly alert as he searched the darkness around them. "I think he'll find us. I wouldn't be surprised if he's out there right now, watching us."

Grace's gaze shot over her shoulder at his words. She shivered as her hand tightened on her purse, the urge to remove her weapon almost overpowering. "Do you really think so?"

He shrugged in response.

Grace released a long breath. "Look, you've really spooked me. Are you sure you'll be all right here alone?"

"He won't make another move tonight. It's too soon."

She frowned. "How do you know that?"

Ethan gazed down at her, bewilderment flashing across his features. "I don't know," he said hoarsely. "I don't know how I know that."

ETHAN WATCHED AS Grace eased her car around the circular drive, then pulled onto the main street. Within moments, the taillights disappeared from his sight, and only then did he walk back into the house, locking the courtyard gate and resetting the alarm behind him. He climbed the staircase again, and for several seconds, stood at the edge of the junglelike room, reluctant to enter.

A deep uneasiness came over him, but he tried to tell himself it was only natural. He had amnesia. He'd almost been killed tonight, and the sister of the woman he'd been having an affair with had all but implicated him in her murder. Why wouldn't he feel uneasy?

But it was more than that. Something other than that. He wondered if his discomfort had more to do with

Grace herself than with her accusations, or even the bizarre situation in which he found himself.

She wasn't telling him everything. He knew instinctively that there was more to Grace Donovan than she'd let on, but Ethan had no idea why he felt this way. He'd seen the grief in her eyes, the pain in her expression when she talked about her sister. He was sure her emotions were genuine, and yet his earlier doubts about her came rushing back. Her reaction was not that of a woman who had just learned of her sister's murder. The guilt, the anger, the obsession to find a loved one's killer were emotions that would come much later.

So what was going on here? Why did Ethan have the feeling that he was a pawn in some very dangerous game?

Was Grace a player, or was she, too, a pawn?

She had explained her relationship with Amy. They hadn't been close. A man had come between them, and they hadn't spoken in years until recently. Until Amy had contacted Grace and told her of the affair with Ethan.

He foraged his mind for a memory of Amy Cole, some remnant of his feelings for her. But there was nothing, and for some reason he couldn't explain, he was almost certain that she'd never meant anything to him.

So was that the kind of person he was? The kind of man who would use a woman for whatever he wanted or needed from her and then discard her without a second thought? Had he done that with his wife?

The cloying scent of the orchids made his head hurt. Ethan hurried out of the room, seeking the shelter of the study he'd found earlier. He didn't want to think about his wife or Amy Cole, and since he didn't remember either of them, it was easy enough to put them out of his mind.

Grace Donovan, however, was a different matter.

At the thought of her, Ethan's uneasiness returned full force, and suddenly he realized where his discomfort was coming from, at least in part. He was attracted to her. He had been from the first.

She wasn't beautiful by any stretch of the imagination, but she was attractive in her own way, and definitely intriguing. And those eyes...

Those eyes could melt a man's soul. He was sure of it.

Her figure wasn't tall and thin, but lush and womanly, and when he'd grabbed her earlier in the hospital parking lot, he'd felt the hardness of her muscles, the toned grace of her body.

If push came to shove, he knew she could hold her own, and that made her all the more alluring. She didn't need taking care of. She didn't need protecting, and that should have rubbed Ethan's male ego the wrong way, but instead it piqued his interest. Made him wonder things he had no business wondering. He was still a married man, even if he couldn't remember his own wife.

He'd left the light on in the office earlier, and now as he entered the room, he tried to put Grace out of his mind and concentrate on his surroundings. There had to be something in here that would trigger a memory for him. Something that would give him a clue as to what he'd been involved in. What had gotten Amy Cole killed.

Slowly, he walked around the room, studying the framed diplomas and certificates that he'd only taken the time to glance at earlier. He'd been educated at

Lover, Stranger

Harvard and Johns Hopkins. He was a board-certified plastic surgeon. He'd received dozens of awards and citations, and had corresponded with dignitaries all over the world.

Among the framed letters on the wall was one from the president of the United States, commending him on his work with underprivileged children born with disfigurements.

Ethan studied his hands. Did he really have the ability to wield a scalpel, the power to change people's lives? Children's lives?

Could that ability and power, all that training and instinct, be subdued by amnesia?

According to the letters and articles, Dr. Ethan Hunter was not only a brilliant surgeon, but a renowned humanitarian. But if he was such a great guy, why the hell was someone trying to kill him?

One whole side of the office contained dozens of framed newspaper articles written about him, but only one carried a photograph. For some reason he couldn't define, Ethan had been reluctant to do more than glance at the picture earlier. He knew it was a photo of him. In spite of the battered condition of his face now, he'd recognized the features. The brown eyes, the dark hair, the angular jaw and chin were the same ones he'd seen in the mirror in Grace's car.

And yet...

The man in the picture was him and it wasn't.

He couldn't explain it any better than that. He didn't feel connected in any way with the image in the photo, and the moment he'd seen it earlier, a dark haze had descended over him. Try as he might, he hadn't been able to compel himself to take that picture from the wall and study it more closely.

He removed it now and carried it with him to the desk, snapping on a brass lamp as he sat down. Placing the picture before him, he fought off a wave of dizziness as he forced himself to look down at his likeness, to study and absorb his own features.

In the photograph, he was standing in front of a white, one-story building with a lush, tropical backdrop. An older, shorter man with a thin, black mustache was in the picture, too, and Ethan's arm was draped over the man's shoulder. They both wore khaki pants and white shirts, both were smiling for the camera, but there was something about Ethan's expression...

Something about the other man's eyes...

He was frightened, Ethan thought suddenly. In spite of the smile and the reassuring arm Ethan had thrown over his shoulder, the mustached man looked scared half to death.

Shaken, Ethan forced himself to read the accompanying article concerning the reopening of the clinic in the Mexican jungle after a half dozen or so *banditos* had destroyed the place once they'd raided it for drugs. The other man in the picture was a Dr. Javier Salizar, a pediatrician who worked full-time at the clinic and who had been on duty the night the *banditos* attacked.

Fortunately, there had been no overnight patients at the hospital. Dr. Salizar had been all alone, and he'd been forced to flee into the jungle and hide until the terrorists had gathered what they wanted and left, burning the clinic to the ground in their wake.

According to the article, Ethan had provided his own personal funds to restore the clinic, and had used his own hands to help rebuild it. He'd spent months of his time getting the clinic operational once again, and the people in the surrounding villages revered him almost like a god.

Ethan didn't understand why, but the article deeply disturbed him. He sensed something bad had happened at that clinic. Something had made him flee, like Dr. Salizar, into the jungle, but not because he had been pursued by *banditos*.

In his dream, Ethan hadn't seen the men chasing him, but he had known just the same that they wore uniforms. They carried guns. He had almost been killed by the Mexican authorities, but Ethan had no idea why.

All he knew was that in some dark and dangerous way, he was tied to that clinic. To that jungle. And the killers that had pursued him in Mexico had followed him here to Houston. To his home.

Hands trembling, Ethan put the picture away and rifled through the paperwork on top of the desk. He turned on the laptop computer and perused the directories, but the files meant nothing. The case studies, medical notations, and patient consultations may as well have been written in a foreign language. Nothing clicked for him. Nothing at all.

Why didn't anything in this office trigger a memory? Why couldn't he remember being a doctor?

Almost frantically, Ethan searched through the desk. At the bottom of a drawer, a gold frame caught his eye. It had been stuffed face-down under a stack of folders. He pulled it out and stared down at a picture of a woman.

This was no snapshot or newspaper clipping, but an elegant studio shot with lighting that complimented the woman's ebony eyes and her full, ruby lips. Thick, glossy black hair had been pulled back to reveal a face as beautiful as it was flawless.

Movie-star glamorous, the woman stood in front of a grand piano, wearing a strapless black evening gown and opera-length, black gloves. Her body was thin, but incredibly shapely. The word that came instantly to mind was statuesque.

She wasn't smiling for the camera, but her lips were parted seductively and her eyes were heavy-lidded and sensual. At the bottom of the picture, scrawled in red ink, were the words: *To my husband, with much love and gratitude, Pilar.*

So this was Ethan's wife. He knew instinctively she'd had the picture made especially for him, and he'd put it away in a drawer face-down.

...the acid...your car...

Ethan stared at the photograph for a very long time, wondering how long they'd been married and what had gone wrong between them. She was an exquisite woman on the surface, but somehow her utter perfection left him cold.

Did I do this to you? he wondered. *Did I make you into this...work of art?*

A work of art without a soul, something told him.

He thought of Grace suddenly, of the unevenness of her features, the short, red hair, the lips that were neither lush nor thin, but in his mind, just right. Her light blue eyes held more life, more mystery, than this woman's ever could.

Disturbed by his thoughts, Ethan put the picture away and closed the drawer. It wasn't fair to give a woman he didn't remember unfavorable attributes in order to justify his attraction to Grace. And that was exactly what he'd been doing.

Had he also tried to justify his affair with Amy Cole? Had there been other women in his marriage?

What kind of husband would treat his wife in such a manner?

What kind of doctor would be pursued through the Mexican jungle by the *policía?*

Ethan wondered if he really wanted to know the answer to any of those questions.

GRACE CLOSED AND locked the door of her hotel room, then slung her jacket toward a chair. Flopping down on the bed, she kicked off her shoes, leaned back against the headboard, then removed her cell phone from her purse and punched in a number she knew by heart.

In spite of the late hour, a woman with a throaty voice answered on the first ring. "Hello?"

"It's Grace."

There was a brief pause before the woman asked, "Are you all right?"

"Amy's dead, Myra."

"Yes, I know."

"What the hell happened tonight?" Grace exploded. "What went wrong?"

"Everything. God, it's all a mess. Hunter wasn't supposed to come back to Houston for at least another two weeks. We would have had plenty of time to set up a sting, but now..." Myra Temple trailed off while she lit up a cigarette. Grace heard her exhale angrily. "As it is, we've rushed the whole operation. We're down here without proper backup or support, and we screwed up. It happens."

"Yes, but this particular screwup cost a woman her life," Grace said angrily. Myra seemed more concerned about the potential damage to the operation than about Amy's death, but that should have come as no surprise. The woman was coldly and consummately professional. Nothing got in her way, and until tonight, Grace had thought she was becoming exactly like her mentor. She'd thought she had the guts to do whatever had to be done to bring a killer to justice.

But after tonight...

"Amy should have been under surveillance. Why wasn't she?"

"She was," Myra snapped. "But somehow she managed to slip through. My guess is that after speaking with us yesterday, she panicked. She had second thoughts about what she'd done, and so she got in touch with Dr. Hunter, probably by cell phone, and warned him that the Feds would be waiting for him when he landed here in Houston. Then she devised a way to get out of her apartment without us knowing."

"How?" Grace demanded.

"Maybe she donned a wig and borrowed her neighbor's car. How the hell should I know? It doesn't help matters that these idiots in the field office down here don't know their butts from a hole in the ground. We can't count on much help in that regard. In any case, Amy appears to have been a lot smarter than I gave her credit for." Myra's tone was a mixture of disgust and admiration.

"So how did Eth—Dr. Hunter manage to get away from us? You were watching the airport yourself."

A loud silence. "He didn't land at Bush Intercontinental Airport," Myra finally said testily, clearly annoyed by Grace's veiled criticism. "I guarantee you, I would have recognized him if he had. We're checking all the private airfields in the area now, but he undoubtedly chartered a plane. Sometime during the flight, he contacted Amy again, and they made plans to meet at the clinic.''

Something in her tone made Grace's heart thud against her chest. ''Myra, you don't think—''

''What?''

Grace tensed. Her hand clutched the tiny cell phone. ''You don't think *he* killed Amy, do you? Because he found out she talked to us?''

Another pause. ''It's possible, but I don't think so. I think he was followed, probably all the way from Mexico, and ambushed at the clinic. I think you and I both know who killed Amy Cole, Grace.''

Grace closed her eyes, dredging up a name from the past. A face from her nightmares. Trevor Reardon. A man who had changed Grace's life forever.

''By the way,'' Myra said softly. ''That was a brilliant stroke on your part—pretending to be Amy's sister.''

More like an act of desperation, Grace thought. Aloud she said, ''Actually, it was Amy's idea. She introduced me to one of her neighbors as her sister. Then she later told me she didn't have any family, but no one in Houston knew that about her because she didn't like to talk about her past.''

When Grace had arrived at the clinic earlier to learn that Amy was dead and Ethan Hunter had been severely beaten, she knew she had to come up with a reason that would put her in close contact with him. And if everything Amy had told her about him was true, Grace was fairly certain Ethan would be wary of the authorities. She couldn't tell him the truth because he would never trust her, never agree to cooperate with her, and so she'd impulsively devised the cover of being Amy's grieving sister. A woman who wanted to find the killer just as badly as Ethan did.

Grace wondered if the ruse had worked, or if like her, he had suspicions.

She ran her fingers through her bangs. "Look, there's another contingency we hadn't counted on. Dr. Hunter now claims he has amnesia."

"Yes, I know," Myra said. "According to his chart, he's suffering some short-term memory loss due to a rather mild concussion."

Grace should have known Myra would have done her homework thoroughly. She'd probably been over Ethan's hospital room with a vacuum.

"I'm afraid it's a little more severe than that," Grace said. "He claims he doesn't remember Amy. Or even his own name, for that matter."

She heard Myra suck in her breath sharply. "You mean he doesn't remember *anything?*"

"That's what he says."

Grace could almost hear the wheels turning in Myra's brain. After a few moments, she said, "Do you think he's faking?"

Grace thought about the darkness and confusion in Ethan's eyes earlier, the desperation that had flashed across his features. Had that been a reaction to what had happened to him in the clinic? Or because he genuinely couldn't remember?

Grace found herself wanting to believe him and that scared her. It was imperative she remain objective. Dispassionate. A consummate professional.

She wondered suddenly what Myra would think if she knew how attracted Grace was to Dr. Ethan Hunter. Would she pull her off the case?

"Well, so what do you think?" Myra's impatient

tone brought Grace out of her reverie, and she realized she'd lapsed into silence for a few seconds too long.

She took a deep breath, willing her tone to remain even. "I thought he might be faking at first. I mean, it seemed a little too coincidental, if Amy did tip him off that we'd be waiting for him. But after spending some time with him tonight, I'm inclined to believe him. He seems genuinely distressed."

Myra's tone was pensive. "So maybe this doesn't have to change anything. Let's think about it for a minute. Whether he's faking or not, your cover should hold up. If Amy told you the truth and she really had no family, there won't be anyone coming out of the woodwork to dispute your claim. And if he *does* have amnesia, it could even work to our advantage. Make him easier to control."

An image of Ethan's bruised and battered face materialized in Grace's mind, and something fluttered in her stomach. Was it pity? Guilt?

Maybe it was just plain old fear, she thought, although for her, that could be the most dangerous emotion of all.

"You aren't having second thoughts about using him, are you?" Myra asked casually, but Grace was immediately on her guard. Was she being tested?

She gripped the phone with grim determination. "Not at all. Ethan Hunter is a means to an end, nothing more."

"Good," Myra said, satisfied. "Because we're getting close, Grace. Can you feel it?"

Grace's stomach knotted with excitement. Or was it dread? "Yes."

"This amnesia thing could be a blessing in disguise, exactly what we need to gain Hunter's cooperation. But we still have to be careful," Myra warned. "Don't do or say anything that will tip him off. I don't have to remind you that one false move and this whole thing could still blow up in our faces."

"Don't worry." Cradling the phone against her shoulder, Grace removed the SIG-Sauer from her purse and released the magazine, pulling back the slide to make sure the gun was unloaded. Then methodically she reloaded the weapon and looked through the sights, relieved to see that her hand was steady, her nerves steeled. "I've waited a long time for this."

"I know you have," Myra said. "But just remember, this can't become a personal vendetta. Once you allow your emotions to get in the way, you become a walking dead woman."

"I understand. You don't have to worry about me. You taught me well."

"I hope so," Myra said softly. "I hope so..."

After they ended the call, Grace poured herself a whiskey over ice and walked out to the tiny balcony of her room. It was still hot. At Ethan's house, the lush tropical foliage, both inside and out, had at least given the illusion of coolness, but here, the heat clung to the concrete and mortar like a desperate lover.

Grace lifted the glass to the back of her neck, letting the cool condensation slide against her skin as the events of the night and remnants of her former life played themselves out in her mind. Funny how one tragic moment, one careless decision could change a person's life forever, could mold you into someone you didn't even recognize anymore.

But tonight she'd glimpsed a bit of the old Grace. Tonight she'd remembered what it was like to be attracted to a man. She'd *felt* something, standing outside with Ethan.

Downing half the contents of her glass, Grace shuddered as the liquid caught fire in her throat and stomach. Myra's warning seemed to reach out from the darkness and taunt her.

Once you allow your emotions to get in the way, you become a walking dead woman.

Chapter Four

The sun streaming in through the tall windows in the third-story master suite awakened Ethan the next morning. He'd tossed and turned for hours the night before, sleeping sporadically, dreaming about running through the jungle and then falling. As in most nightmares, he never remembered hitting the ground but instead would awaken abruptly in a cold sweat, his heart pounding, adrenaline still rushing through his veins.

He sat up now and looked around, slowly letting the events of last evening filter back in. He'd hoped that by morning his memory would have returned, but his mind was still pretty much a blank. He still had no idea who Ethan Hunter really was, what he might have done, or why someone wanted to kill him. All he knew for sure was that he had to somehow keep it together. He had to remain sharp until he could find out what the hell was going on.

His body aching, he pulled himself out of bed and headed for the shower. Like the bedroom, the master bath was huge and luxurious, with lush, green carpeting, intricate tile mosaics, a step-up marble bathtub, and a shower stall that could easily accommodate two.

Turning on the water in the shower, Ethan stood staring at his reflection in the mirror over the double vanity. The bruises on his face were still prominent, but the swelling had gone down, and the pain wasn't quite so severe. He almost looked human this morning, although his face was still one he didn't recognize.

Stripping away the last of his clothing, he examined the appendectomy scar on his lower right side. The wound was surprisingly large, about four inches long, and still tender to the touch. Ethan stared at the scar, trying to remember the surgery, but nothing came to him. Nothing but the fleeting memory of being pursued through the jungle. The echoing sound of gunfire. The lingering unease that Dr. Ethan Hunter was a man he wasn't sure he wanted to get to know.

Ignoring the twinges of pain from the cuts and bruises, he stepped under the hot water, washing briskly, trying to elude the questions whirling inside his head by concentrating on the mundane. Showering. Getting dressed. Finding something to eat.

Back in the bedroom, he gazed at the clothing hanging in the massive walk-in closet. The expensive suits and custom-made shirts were as unfamiliar to him as the face he'd studied in the bathroom mirror.

Finally, randomly, he grabbed something casual, a pair of charcoal pants and a cotton knit pullover. The pants were loose in the waist, and he wondered if he'd lost weight after his surgery. The shirt fit fine, but the shoes he pulled from the closet were a little snug. He started to find another pair, but then froze when he heard a noise. Somewhere downstairs a door opened and closed.

It occurred to Ethan that Rosa might have come back, but she'd said last night that today was her day off. She planned to spend the time with her daughter. So who was downstairs then?

Ethan scanned the room for a weapon. His eyes lit on the nightstand next to the bed, and he crossed the floor to search through the drawers. If he kept a gun in the house, he reasoned that would be the logical place for it, but his search was fruitless.

Removing the shade from the heavy brass lamp on the night stand, Ethan jerked the plug from the wall and picked up the base. As a weapon, it was cumbersome at best, but he didn't have time to look for anything else. Whoever was in the house might even now be slipping up the stairs to ambush him.

Heart thumping, his senses on full alert, Ethan left the bedroom, making his way toward the stairs. He paused on the landing, peering over the railing into the jungle-like living room below him. Nothing moved. No sound came to him.

In sock feet, he slipped silently down the stairs, his gaze searching every nook and corner of the room. There were any number of places an intruder could hide, but the most obvious place seemed to be the study. The door was ajar, and Ethan was almost certain he'd closed it last night before going to bed.

He crossed the room and flattened himself against the wall outside the study, listening. From inside, he could detect shuffling sounds, as if someone was going through his papers.

Nerves pumped, Ethan glanced inside. And tensed.

A woman stood before an open safe, busily removing what looked to be bundles of cash. He recognized her immediately from the picture he'd found in the desk last night. The intruder was his wife.

She didn't see him at first. Ethan watched her for

several seconds as she stood at the safe. The red suit she wore was so short and so tight that she didn't appear to be armed, but the thought crossed Ethan's mind that she was probably extremely dangerous anyway. A woman scorned could be deadly.

He set the brass lamp on the floor, then stepped into the room. Her head jerked toward the door, her hand flying to her heart when she saw him. She blinked once, then twice before she finally managed to get her shock under control. "Ethan!" Her voice was lyrical and very feminine, traced with a Spanish accent. "I didn't know you were home."

Ethan glanced at the bundles of cash. "I can see that."

She made no move to close the safe door, nor to hide the money she'd stacked on top of his desk. Instead she took one of the bundles and brazenly thumbed through the bills. "I heard you were in the hospital." Glancing up, her gaze flicked over his bruised features. Something flashed in her eyes, an emotion Ethan couldn't define. "You look and sound terrible," she said.

"Thanks." He returned her perusal, taking a long moment to study her features, and decided that the photograph in his desk, as spectacular as it was, didn't do her justice. She was even more beautiful in person. The deep V-neck of her jacket revealed a magnificent cleavage while the impossibly short skirt highlighted impossibly long legs.

But what drew Ethan's attention more than her grace and sultry beauty was the fact that she appeared to be stealing him blind.

As if reading his mind, she glanced down at the

money and shrugged. "It's not like you don't owe me."

When he didn't protest, she gave him an odd glance, then turned back to the safe. Her hair cascaded down her back, almost to her waist, gleaming like ebony when she tossed it over her shoulder.

"What are you doing here anyway?" she asked, her voice muffled as she reached inside the safe. "Bob said you'd been beaten up pretty badly. He thought you'd be in the hospital for several more days." She withdrew another packet of bills, then turned to face him, her dark eyes challenging.

"Bob who?" Ethan asked, without thinking.

She arched a perfect black brow. "Bob Kendall. Your ex-partner, remember? Who else would I be talking about?"

Ethan was immediately on his guard. Kendall was his ex-partner? If the hostility in the man's eyes last night had been any indication, the arrangement had ended badly. Ethan wondered what had gone wrong, in his business and in his marriage.

He stared at his wife, trying to dredge up a memory, some leftover emotion, but nothing came to him. Nothing but a faint uneasiness as he watched her.

"When did you talk to Bob?" he asked.

Something that might have been guilt flashed over her features. She began stuffing the money into a large black tote bag. "He called me last night. He was at the hospital when you were brought in, and he thought I'd want to know what happened."

Ethan remembered what Rosa had told him last evening, that Pilar had called here at the house because Kendall had told her Ethan was returning. Why? he wondered. There had been none of her clothing in the closet upstairs, no makeup or feminine toiletries in the bathroom. It was obvious she no longed lived here, so why had she called Rosa to find out when he was returning?

And why wait until he got back to rob his safe? Unless, of course, things hadn't gone according to plan—

Had Pilar and Kendall been behind Ethan's attack last night? Had they somehow arranged for him to go to the clinic before coming home? Had they wanted to kill him?

Ethan studied his wife and wondered why that notion didn't seem preposterous to him. Was it because Pilar Hunter struck him as a woman who would get what she wanted no matter who she had to hurt in the process?

But she was also a woman Ethan had married, must have once loved. He wondered how he could feel nothing, not even anger, toward her now.

Her task completed, she closed the bag and slung the straps over her shoulder. She walked around the desk and started by him, then paused. "Bob told me about Amy. I guess I should say I'm sorry."

Ethan said nothing.

For the first time, he sensed an uncertainty about his wife, as if she didn't know whether to say more or end it here and now. Then she smiled. "I never believed you loved her, you know. Not like you once loved me." Gazing up at him, she lifted a hand to his face.

Ethan resisted the urge to step back from her. Instead he held his ground, letting her place a cool palm against his bruised skin. For one long moment, he stared down at her perfect features, her incredible beauty, and wondered again why he felt nothing.

And she knew. Like a lightning bolt, anger whipped across her features. *"Cabrón,"* she muttered as she turned and brushed by him. Outside the doorway, she glanced back. "You do look terrible, you know. Besides the bruises, I mean. You've lost weight. Your eyes…" she trailed off, studying him.

"What about my eyes?" he asked sharply.

"They're cold. Even colder than I remembered." She shuddered. "You are not the man I married, Ethan. You haven't been for a very long time."

WHEN GRACE ARRIVED at the house a little while later, she was amazed to see how much better Ethan looked. Even though the bruises hadn't faded, the swelling in his face had gone down so that his features were no longer distorted. She could tell more clearly what he looked like, and when he'd first opened the door, she'd caught her breath in surprise.

"I…hope I didn't get you up," she said, her gaze slipping over him. He was dressed, but his hair was mussed and he wasn't wearing any shoes. His casualness made her feel stuffy in her beige pantsuit, silk shell and brown flats.

"I've been up for a while," he said, his voice still hoarse. He stood back so she could enter. Grace stepped past him into the foyer, then waited while he closed the door and reactivated the alarm.

"Have you remembered anything?" she asked anxiously.

He gave her a look. "You don't waste any time, do you?"

Grace shrugged. "Why should I? Someone out there killed my sister last night, and he may come back to finish you off. Who has time for formalities?"

"I get your point," he said dryly. "And the answer to your question is, no. I haven't remembered anything."

"Nothing at all?"

"Nothing that makes any sense."

Grace glanced up at him, trying to read his expression. "Well, if it's any consolation, you look much better today. Almost like a different man."

"So I've already been told." He turned and started for the stairs.

"By whom?" Grace asked quickly. "Has someone been here this morning?"

He paused on the bottom step, turning to glance over his shoulder. "My wife was here earlier. I caught her taking money out of the safe in the study."

Grace frowned. "What do you mean, you *caught* her?"

"Just that. Apparently she no longer lives here. But I guess she decided to come back and help herself to whatever cash I might have left lying around."

Grace took a moment to assess this new information. So Ethan had met Pilar Hunter face to face. Grace couldn't help wondering how the meeting had gone, or what he'd thought of the woman. What he'd felt for her. From the pictures Grace had seen, Pilar was an incredibly beautiful woman.

Absently, Grace ran a hand down her pantsuit, smoothing invisible wrinkles. "So what was it like seeing her?" she tried to ask casually. "Did she give you any clues about your relationship? About what might have happened between the two of you?"

Ethan paused. "I don't have any idea what happened between us, but I'll tell you one thing. She struck me as a woman perfectly capable of throwing acid on my car. Or in my face, for that matter.''

The bluntness of his words threw Grace for a moment. ''Do you think she may have had something to do with Amy's death?''

''I wouldn't rule out the possibility,'' he said grimly. He turned and started up the stairs. ''Come on up. We can talk about this later. I've located the kitchen, and I'm cooking breakfast.''

Grace followed him up the stairs and through the living room. The parrot, fully awake and preening on his perch, let out a loud squawk when he saw her.

''Don't even start,'' she muttered.

''What?'' Ethan said over his shoulder.

''I said that's a good start. Learning your way around the house, I mean.''

He gave her a quizzical look, then led her through a dining room with a high ceiling and a magnificent stained glass window, into the kitchen, with its stainless steel appliances, satillo tile floor, and wall of atrium doors that gave a broad view of a backyard pool and waterfall.

Ethan walked over to the range and dished up a plate of bacon and eggs, then added a pile of buttered toast. ''Have you eaten? There's plenty for both of us.''

Grace eyed the food longingly. She'd started the day with her usual meal, one half of a grapefruit and a cup of coffee. If she ate bacon and eggs, she'd have to add at least half an hour to her daily workout in the gym, not to mention an extra mile or two to her run. For a moment, she considered that it might be worth it. She hadn't had a piece of bacon in ages.

Willpower, she reminded herself. She had to remain

sharp both physically and mentally. "Just a glass of orange juice for me."

He poured them both a glass of juice from a pitcher he removed from the refrigerator, then carried his food to the breakfast table. Grace followed him. He took the seat facing the atrium doors and outside, while Grace sat across from him, with a clear view of the kitchen door. She kept her purse on her lap.

For a few moments, neither of them said anything. Ethan ate ravenously, as if he hadn't had a solid meal in days. Grace tried not to stare at him, but his looks had changed so dramatically overnight, she couldn't help studying his features.

When he caught her watching him, she said, "I can't get over the changes in your appearance. It's amazing."

He shrugged. "There was a lot of room for improvement. I looked pretty horrible last night."

"I didn't mean it like that," Grace said. "You must be a really fast healer, that's all."

"Maybe." A shadow flickered over his features, and Grace wondered what he was thinking. If he was remembering something. She couldn't help wondering what he'd been like before all this happened. Would he have been the kind of man she would have wanted to spend time with? Doubtful, if everything Amy had told her was true.

"Were you able to get some sleep last night?" she asked him.

He grimaced. "Some. I'm still not used to this place. It...doesn't feel like home to me, but I guess that's to be expected, considering."

Grace nodded. "It'll take time. I gather you've done some exploring this morning."

"I've been over this place from top to bottom. Nothing triggered a memory. But at least I did find the kitchen. And a gym downstairs. I want to start working out as soon as possible. Build back my strength."

Grace's gaze dropped to his broad shoulders and chest, the muscular arms bulging beneath the short sleeves of his shirt. She remembered the strength in those arms last night when he'd grabbed her, the hardness of his chest when he'd held her against him. If he was out of shape, she could only imagine what he would be like at his peak. "You don't want to rush it," she said. "Amy said you'd had surgery recently. An appendectomy, I believe."

"That's what I've been told, but I don't remember the surgery, either. Although I do have a scar on my side." Again his features momentarily darkened, as if he'd suddenly remembered something he had no intention of sharing. Grace wondered what he was keeping from her.

"Tell me more about your meeting with Pilar," she said.

The cloud over his features changed, but didn't fade. "Not much to tell. Like I said, I found her in the study taking money out of the safe."

"Did she say why she was doing that?"

Ethan pushed aside his plate as if his appetite had suddenly deserted him. He glanced up. "She seemed to think I owed her."

"Because of Amy?"

He shrugged.

"I've seen pictures of Pilar." Grace paused. "She's a very beautiful woman."

"Yes, she certainly is."

"Did you, you know, *feel* anything when you saw her?"

One dark brow rose at the question. "You mean attraction?"

"I'm just trying to figure out what your relationship with her is," Grace said, almost defensively.

"Like I said earlier, apparently we're separated. She wasn't here long enough for me to find out much of anything, but she did mention Amy. She knew about the shooting."

Grace glanced at him in surprise. "What did she say?"

He shrugged. "Let me put it this way. I don't think Amy's death came exactly as a blow."

Something that might have been sympathy crossed his features, and Grace lowered her eyes. Even though her deception was necessary, it didn't make it any easier. "How did she find out about Amy's death?"

"Do you remember Rosa mentioning a man named Kendall? She said that Pilar had called to find out what time I would be home, because Dr. Kendall had told her I was arriving last night. Kendall was at the hospital when I was brought in. He was in my room when I came to. Evidently he called Pilar and told her what happened."

Grace thought about that for a moment. "Do you know anything about this Kendall?"

"Only that he's my ex-partner."

Grace paused. "Do you think Pilar and Dr. Kendall might have something going on?"

Ethan's expression didn't waver. "I wondered about that. I've also wondered why Pilar waited until I got back to come here and take money from the safe. According to the police detective I spoke with last night,

I was in Mexico for weeks, recovering from the surgery. She could have come over here at any time and taken that money. Why wait until I got back?''

Grace frowned. ''What are you getting at?''

''Well, just think about it for a minute.'' He toyed with the juice glass. ''Why would she wait until now to take that money out of the safe?''

''Maybe she didn't need it until now.''

''Exactly,'' Ethan said. ''Because maybe all along she thought there would be a lot more where that came from.'' His gaze went past Grace to focus on the backyard. She didn't turn, but she could hear the faint tinkling of the waterfall cascading into the pool, and she wondered if he was thinking about the jungle. Why did he seem to have such an aversion to it?

''After Pilar left this morning, I went through the safe myself,'' Ethan finally said. ''I found a life insurance policy for five million dollars that named her as the beneficiary. I'd be willing to bet that's a lot more than she took out of the safe.''

''So what exactly are you saying, Ethan? That Pilar was behind what happened to you last night? You think she tried to have you killed?''

His gaze met Grace's. ''I don't know why that surprises you. You said yourself last night this whole thing may be a *Fatal Attraction* in reverse. Don't you think a woman is capable of murder?''

Grace thought about the killer she wanted to bring to justice, felt the weight of her own gun in her purse. ''Yes,'' she said grimly. ''I know there are women who are very capable of killing. Who might even take pleasure from it. But as I also told you last night, from the things Amy told me, I don't think Pilar is the one who wants you dead. Or at least, I don't think she's the one who tried to have you killed.''

Her distinction was not lost on Ethan. His gaze on her cooled. "You were pretty clear in that regard. You think I did something to set last night's events in motion. You think someone is trying to kill me because of something I did in Mexico. Something illegal.''

His voice was hard, unyielding, but Grace sensed an undercurrent of anguish. A hint of desperation in his tone. She shrugged. "Look, I'm just going by Amy's letters—''

"Amy's *letters*," he said, shoving back his chair and standing. "Amy *said*." He strode to the atrium doors and stood staring out into the sunlit garden. "I know she was your sister, and I'm sorry she's dead, but I don't remember her, and from what you told me last night, you didn't know her that well, either. What if everything she told you about me was a lie? What if she was setting me up somehow?''

Grace turned in her chair to stare at him. "You don't really believe that.''

"Why is it so hard to believe?'' His jaw hardened as he turned to face her. "Why is it so easy for you to believe that I was involved in something that got her killed? You don't know me. What do you really know about me?''

Before Grace could answer, he walked back over to the table and stood staring down at her. The look in his eyes made her shiver. "And it suddenly occurs to me,'' he said slowly, "that I don't know anything about you, either.''

"Of course, you do,'' Grace said, ignoring the tiny spark of panic that flared inside her. She stood, trying to take away his advantage, trying to regain control of the situation as she met his gaze and they squared off.

His eyes narrowed on her. "What do I know about you? Your name? That you're Amy's sister? I know those things because *you* told me."

Grace moistened her lips. "What are you driving at?"

"Maybe I've been a little too trusting. Maybe I should have asked a few more questions last night."

"Ask them now," Grace said, her voice growing cold. "I'll tell you anything you want to know."

The silence in the kitchen was deafening. When he spoke, his voice was almost too calm. "Who do you work for?"

Grace's heart thumped against her chest. She fingered the gold clasp of her purse. "Don't you mean *where* do I work? I work for a legal firm."

"You're a lawyer?"

She shook her head. "I went to law school, but I never took the bar exam. I'm more of a...researcher."

"What does that mean?"

"It means I spend a lot of time behind a computer and doing legwork for my superiors. There's a lot of grunt work involved in what I do."

He paused again. "You don't have an accent," he accused. "How long have you lived in Houston?"

She answered without hesitation. "Not long. I transferred down here from Washington, D.C."

"What did you do there?"

"Same thing."

"Why did you move to Houston?"

"To be near my sister." That was the first outright lie she'd told him all morning, but Grace knew there would be plenty of others. She'd say and do whatever she had to in order to gain his trust. That was the way she'd been trained. The way she lived her life. She couldn't afford to get an attack of conscience now simply because a man with a battered face and a hidden past was awakening feelings inside her she had thought were long dead.

"What about your family?" he asked. "Where are they?"

"My parents have been dead for years." Without warning, the old memory came storming back. Grace thought she had buried it, along with her emotions, someplace safe, someplace impenetrable, but all of a sudden it was back, the explosion in her mind as shattering as the one that night had been.

In the beat of a heart, she was a teenager again, running down the street toward the sirens. Seeing the fire licking red-orange against the night sky. Hearing the screams of the people trapped inside the white frame house. Her mother and father. And at an upstairs window, beating against the panes, her hair in flames, Grace's sister. Her beautiful, beautiful sister...

"Everyone is gone," she whispered. Ethan touched her hand, and Grace jumped, forgetting for a moment where she was. Who she was supposed to be. She stared up at him, fighting back the scream that tore at her throat. The horror that had made her who and what she was.

"I'm sorry," he said. His eyes, cold and suspicious before, were now clouded with guilt. It was hard for Grace to witness that guilt, knowing what she knew.

He's not innocent, she told herself. *Don't be fooled.*

She opened her purse and withdrew her wallet, showing him her driver's license, her social security card, and then fishing out a business card that contained the name and address of a downtown law firm. The business cards had been printed overnight. The address and phone number had been supplied by the field office here in Houston.

"You can call them if you like," she said, handing the card to Ethan. The call would be forwarded to either Myra or a support operative who would bear out Grace's story. If Ethan actually went by the office, the receptionist would refer him to one of the partners who had been briefed and would know how to field the inquiry. "But I am who I say I am. My name is Grace Donovan, and I am looking for my sister's killer."

He nodded, as if he'd seen something in her face that had convinced him. He sat down at the table, looking as if the remainder of his strength had suddenly drained away. "Did you bring Amy's letters with you today?"

Grace sat down beside him. She could smell the faint scent of soap and shampoo, and wondered if, like her, he'd spent a long time in the shower that morning, trying to scrub away the past. Or what he feared might be there.

"No, but I brought this." She pulled a newspaper clipping from her purse, and placed it face up before him. The article was accompanied by a picture of a blond man who looked to be in his early thirties.

Grace stared long and hard at that picture, then turned away, shuddering. "I found that clipping in Amy's apartment one day. When I asked her, she denied knowing anything about it, but I could tell she was upset. Frightened. She'd cut this picture out of the paper for a reason, but she wouldn't tell me why."

Ethan picked up the clipping and scanned the article.

"Trevor Reardon," he read, then glanced up. "It says he's on the FBI's Ten Most Wanted List."

Grace nodded. "He was convicted on three counts of first-degree murder and sentenced to life in prison without parole. He escaped several months ago and has been underground ever since."

"So what does this have to do with me?" Ethan asked.

"You don't recognize him? Look closely." As he examined the picture of Trevor Reardon, Grace studied Ethan's features, looking for a flicker, any telltale sign of recognition.

After several seconds, he handed the clipping back to her. "I don't recognize him. Am I supposed to?"

"Are you sure?" Grace asked anxiously.

"As far as I know, I've never seen this man before." Ethan's voice was edged with impatience. "And I don't think I like what you're implying."

"I'm not implying anything—"

"The hell you're not. What connection do you think I have to a convicted murderer? Just what kind of man do you think I am?"

"I don't know," she said softly, her gaze meeting his in defiance. "Isn't that what we're both trying to find out?"

For a long moment, his gaze held hers, then he glanced away. Running both hands through his hair, he stared at the ceiling. "What connection do you think I have to this Trevor Reardon?" he asked again.

Grace paused. "I think you may have given him a new face."

Chapter Five

Ethan stared at her as if she'd taken leave of her senses. Then, as the full meaning of her words sank in, he stared at her in horror. "Why would I do that?" He was a doctor, for God's sake. A humanitarian, according to the articles and awards in his office. Why would he knowingly give a murderer a new face, a new life?

Something that almost looked like sympathy flashed across Grace's face before she could subdue it. In the blink of an eye, however, the mask was back in place. She stared at him dispassionately. "It's possible you were somehow coerced."

"But that's not what you think, is it?"

She hesitated, her gaze resting briefly on the picture of Trevor Reardon's face, then lifting to Ethan's. Any trace of sympathy she might have felt earlier had vanished. "No. I think you did it for money," she said bluntly.

"But why would I?" he demanded. "Look at this place. These clothes. It's obvious I already have money."

When Grace said nothing, he grabbed her hand and stood, drawing her to her feet. "Come with me."

"What? Where?" Her voice sounded almost panicky. She grabbed her purse and slung the strap over her shoulder.

Without another word, Ethan pulled her out of the kitchen, through the dining room and living room toward the study. The parrot gave a weak little squawk as they hurried passed him, but Ethan ignored him.

Inside the study, he walked to the middle of the room and gestured to all the framed awards and citations on the walls. "Look at all this stuff." He walked over and took one of the framed letters down, then held it out to Grace. "Do you know what this is? It's a letter from the president of the United States commending me on my work in Mexico. This one is from a senator, this one from our ambassador to Mexico." He went on and on, until he'd taken a half dozen or so frames from the wall and piled them in Grace's arms.

Apparently unimpressed, she stacked them on his desk.

Ethan knew his movements were almost frantic as he removed another frame from the wall, but he couldn't help himself. He had to convince her, and himself, that what she was thinking was ludicrous. "Why would somebody who has done all this work for underprivileged children, received all these accolades, risk losing everything by changing a murderer's face?"

"Because all that philanthropy takes a great deal of money, and you also have very expensive tastes." Grace made a sweeping gesture with her hand. "You can't buy all this with citations and awards and letters from the president. Plus, you have the perfect cover. Your clinic in Mexico is remote, practically inaccessible, from what Amy said, and perfectly legitimate."

"Except for the fact that, according to you, I operate on criminals on the side," he said bitterly. "I give them new faces so they're free to go out into the world to rape, murder, and steal at will.''

Grace's gaze didn't quite meet his. ''Reardon probably found out about you from someone in prison. When he escaped, he made his way across the border and somehow found your clinic in the jungle. I think he gave you a great deal of money, probably millions, to give him a new face.''

''Millions?'' Ethan frowned. ''The article said he'd been in prison for over six years. Where would he get that kind of money?''

''At the time he was caught, it was estimated that he'd amassed a fortune worth well over thirty million dollars. It was never found.''

Ethan stared at her in surprise. ''So who is this guy anyway?''

Grace paused. ''He's an ex-Navy SEAL and an explosives expert who sold his services to the highest bidder. He became a mercenary, an assassin, sometimes a terrorist. It didn't much matter to him what the job entailed so long as the price was right. He enjoyed killing and he was good at it. It was all a game to him, one he made a lot of money from. The first time he escaped prison, he went after the FBI agent who had captured him. Reardon firebombed the agent's house and wired all the doors to explode when the people trapped inside or the rescuers on the outside tried to open them. There was no way in or out. The agent, his wife and a daughter all died in the fire.''

Her expression remained coldly dispassionate, but Ethan sensed she wasn't quite as calm as she appeared. There were lights inside her eyes. Tiny flares of rage when she spoke. Was she thinking of her sister?

''After that, he remained free for several years,''

Grace said. "He was a master of disguises, always staying one step ahead of the authorities. He may even have gone out of the country for a while. But then he made one very serious mistake. The only one in the agent's family who hadn't been killed in the fire was a teenage girl who'd sneaked out of the house that night. Reardon came back to get her."

"Why?" Ethan asked. "How could the girl hurt him?"

"Because she could identify him, for one thing. And because she was a loose end. From everything I've learned about Reardon, he doesn't like loose ends. He's almost obsessive about it."

"So what happened when he came back for the girl?"

"There was another agent, a woman. She was the murdered agent's partner. She'd made it her life's work to track down Reardon and send him back to prison. She knew he'd eventually come after the girl, and when he did, she got him."

Ethan didn't much like the sound of that. "You mean she used the girl as bait?"

Grace shrugged. "That's one way of putting it. But she also saved the girl's life. To her, the end justified the means." Grace picked up one of the framed citations and studied it closely.

Ethan used the opportunity to study her. She seemed as focused as ever this morning, her voice steady, her expression still as determined as he remembered it.

But what he hadn't remembered was how the blue of her eyes lightened or darkened depending on her emotions, or how the tint of her lip gloss reminded him of lush, ripe strawberries. What he hadn't remembered was the scent of her perfume, so subtle it seemed hardly more than imagination, or the way her modestly cut jacket only hinted at the womanly curves beneath. Ethan hadn't remembered any of those things—or was it that he had just been working very hard to forget them?

"How do you know so much about this Reardon?" he asked her.

They both glanced up at the same time, their gazes locking. Ethan's gaze was drawn to her lips when she spoke. "A lot of the information is in the article I showed you, plus, after I found that clipping in Amy's apartment, I did some research. I wanted to know why Reardon's picture seemed to frighten her so much."

"You think Amy knew what was going on in the Mexican clinic?"

"I think she at least suspected, and that's why she was so afraid." Grace set aside the frame she'd been holding. "Amy had been to the clinic with you on at least one occasion. She even alluded to the fact that she'd seen a man down there, a patient, whose face was covered in bandages. She didn't know who he was, but she found his presence at the clinic strange because most of your patients down there are children. I think she came back here and somehow started putting two and two together."

Ethan walked over and stared at the picture of him and Dr. Salizar in front of the Mexican Clinic. If everything Grace said was true, no wonder Salizar looked so frightened. Ethan wondered if the clinic had really been burned to the ground by *banditos,* or if one of his former patients had come back looking for him.

He turned to Grace. "So you think Reardon killed Amy because she was on to him?"

"No. I think Amy was a bonus. I think you were the

target because you may be the only person in the world who has seen Trevor Reardon's new face.''

In spite of himself, Ethan felt chilled by her words. ''And now I can't identify him because I don't remember him.''

''That's the ironic part,'' Grace said. ''He could be anyone. Your next-door neighbor. The mailman. Anyone. If Trevor Reardon wants you dead, the only way you can survive is to somehow find him first.''

''You mean use myself as bait,'' Ethan said, marveling at her coolness. ''Like the FBI agent used the girl.''

Grace shrugged. ''It makes sense. You're a loose end. Sooner or later, Reardon will come after you.''

''And when he does?''

She shrugged again. ''When he does, we have to be ready for him.''

He looked at her and just shook his head. ''Has it ever once occurred to you that you and I are hardly trained to capture a murderer, let alone an ex-Navy SEAL who has a penchant for explosives?'' For a moment, Ethan thought she was actually going to smile at his words. She almost seemed to be enjoying herself, and he said angrily, ''For God's sake, this isn't a game, Grace. I'm a plastic surgeon without a memory, and you're a—what did you call it—a researcher for a law firm? What in the hell makes you think we can pull this off?''

''Have you got a better plan?'' she demanded. ''You certainly can't go to the police.''

Ethan closed his eyes briefly, remembering the jungle, the fear, the certainty that the men who pursued him *were* the police. Had the Mexican authorities been on to him? Was that why he'd been running?

If what Grace suspected was true, if Ethan had in fact aided and abetted criminals by selling them new faces, then he would more than likely be looking at a stiff sentence of his own if he were to go to the police. And maybe, if he had done all the things Grace thought he had, prison was exactly where he should be.

But there was still some doubt in Ethan's mind, still some lingering suspicion that Grace Donovan hadn't told him everything. That she had left out something very important, and until he could figure out the whole story, he wasn't about to throw himself on the mercy of the court.

"Maybe I can't go to the police," he said. "But I still don't understand what's stopping you."

"I thought I explained myself last night."

"But it still doesn't make sense. I don't want to seem cruel, but you can't help your sister by getting yourself killed. If I'm Trevor Reardon's target, then I don't want you anywhere near me."

"Don't be ridiculous," Grace said, frowning. "You can't do this alone. You need me. I can watch your back. We can watch each other's back for that matter, because I'm not giving up on this. Reardon killed my sister, and I'm going to make damned sure he pays. If you won't help me, I'll go after him on my own."

And she would do it, Ethan thought. He could see the determination in her eyes, in the defiant way she held her chin and jaw. She would go after Reardon alone, and then Ethan would have *her* death on his conscience.

The thought of her getting hurt or killed made him almost physically sick. "You don't know what you're getting yourself into," he said.

She lifted her chin. "Yes, I do. I'm not helpless. Believe me, I can take care of myself."

"Against an assassin-turned-terrorist?"

Her gaze flickered but didn't waver. "He's a man. He has weaknesses. We know two things about him. He's dangerous and he's compulsive. He won't be able to resist coming back to finish what he started. All we have to do is be ready for him."

She made it sound so easy, but somehow Ethan knew she wasn't being naive. She really believed what she was saying, and her confidence was almost enough to convince him. Almost.

"So what's our first move?" he asked.

Sunlight from the window fired the red highlights in her hair as she tucked a strand behind her ear. "I guess the best way to flush him out is to go about your normal business. If Reardon is after you, then he's probably made a point of knowing your routine."

"I hope you're not suggesting I see patients today," Ethan said dryly. "I don't think I'm up for that. And I don't think they would be, either."

"No, of course not," Grace said. "But you can always check in with your office, maybe even go by there. After that, we'll play it by ear."

He said suddenly, "Do you have a key to Amy's apartment?"

"No, why?"

"Because you found one clue there already. Maybe there are others."

"You don't think the police will have cordoned off her apartment?"

Ethan shook his head. "Not likely. From what the detective told me last night, they're inclined to believe someone broke into the office looking for drugs, and

Amy was shot when she surprised him. The police will be canvassing the neighborhood this morning, looking for witnesses and evidence dropped or stashed by the suspect. They may never feel the need to search Amy's apartment.''

Grace mulled that over. "You're probably right. Like I said, I don't have a key, but I can get us in.''

That confidence again. Ethan stared at her admiringly. "All right. You can make yourself at home down here while I go up and finish dressing. Then we can get out of here.''

UPSTAIRS, ETHAN HURRIED over to the nightstand by the bed and opened the top drawer, removing the stack of bills he'd found in the safe that Pilar had somehow missed. Then he picked up the pistol he'd found in the safe. The gun was small, a high-caliber, custom-made job that almost fit inside Ethan's hand.

He tested the weight of the gun as a strong sense of déjà vu slipped over him. He'd had that same feeling the moment his hand had closed over the weapon in the safe. It was the first thing he'd come across that had seemed familiar to him since waking up in the hospital last evening.

Ethan knew how to use the gun. Not just a gun, but this particular gun. He knew the sights would be accurate, the trigger pull crisp and the recoil minimal. He couldn't even remember his own mother, and yet he knew how to field strip this weapon and reassemble it in a matter of seconds.

Trying not to think about what that might mean, he slammed back the slide to put one bullet in the chamber, flipped on the safety with his thumb, then slipped the pistol into the back waistband of his pants. Next he peeled away several bills from the wad of money and stuffed them in his pocket. The rest he returned to the drawer.

The shoes he'd been wearing the night before were beside the bed where he'd kicked them off. He slid them on, thinking briefly how much better they fit than the ones he'd tried on earlier that morning. His final preparation was to grab a jacket from the closet. It would be hot outside, but he needed something to conceal his gun. No use revealing *all* his secrets to Grace. Not yet at least.

As he walked down the stairs to join her, Ethan couldn't help reflecting on how much better he felt with money in his pocket and a high-powered weapon within his reach.

Just what the hell kind of doctor was he anyway?

THEY DROVE SOUTH on Gessner Road, a long street that was beautiful in some areas and cluttered with shopping centers, convenience stores and apartment buildings in others. The section near Ethan's house was particularly lovely, with its tree-shaded sidewalks and flower-strewn median.

The abundance of towering oaks and loblolly pines was one of the things that had surprised Grace most about Houston. She had expected a dry, sprawling metropolis dotted with oil wells and ugly refineries, but the city was very wooded with houses and glass office buildings almost hidden beneath thick canopies of green.

Out of the corner of her eye, she saw Ethan staring out the window, watching the road signs, trying to familiarize himself with the city. For a moment, she tried to put herself in his place, but it was impossible to imagine what he was going through. To have no recall of who you were, what kind of person you'd been, but to have every reason to suspect the worst. To have been told everything he'd been told that morning—

Grace nudged away the guilt prodding at her conscience. Everything she'd done was necessary. Every lie and deception essential. She wouldn't spend time regretting what couldn't be helped.

Crossing Westheimer, one of the main thoroughfares in Houston, she turned right on Richmond, then pulled into an apartment group called The Pines.

The complex was like a number of others they'd passed along the way—two-story buildings that housed between four and eight "garden" apartments per unit. The grounds were immaculately groomed, with huge pink and white oleander bushes hugging the sides of the buildings while tall pine trees, circled by beds of impatiens and monkey grass, shaded the common grounds between the units.

Grace parked in front of the leasing office, shut off the engine, and turned to Ethan. In spite of the trees, the intense heat and sultry humidity invaded the car. She lowered the windows, but without a breeze, it didn't help much.

"Maybe you'd better let me go in alone," she said. "I don't want to make anyone suspicious."

She saw from his expression that he understood her meaning. Though improved, his bruised appearance was still enough to raise eyebrows. He nodded and watched her open the car door. Grace felt his eyes on her until she disappeared inside the office.

As always, the air conditioning hit her full blast. That was something else Grace had yet to get used to—going from a furnace to a freezer in a matter of seconds. Houstonians seemed to think they could compensate for the soaring temperatures outside by turning their AC to frigid. Even wearing a jacket, Grace found herself shivering.

A woman with frosted blonde hair sat reading a book behind a large desk near the doorway. The red-and-blue rhinestones on her T-shirt sparkled in the overhead lighting as she reached up and removed her glasses. "May I help you?"

Grace walked over and stood in front of the desk. "I hope so. My name is Grace Donovan. One of your tenants is…was…my sister." She broke off and glanced down at her hands. After a split second, she said, "Her name was Amy Cole. She lived in 4C."

The woman's gaze grew anxious. "You said, was."

Grace bit her lip. "She was killed last night."

The woman gasped. Her manicured fingers flew to her fuchsia-stained lips. "I'm so sorry. H-how did it happen?"

Grace released a long, shaky breath. "I can't really go into the details right now. It's…still so fresh. I'm sure you understand."

"Of course." The woman was at a loss. She stared helplessly at Grace. "Is there anything I can do?"

"As a matter of fact, yes. I need to get into Amy's apartment."

A frown flitted across the woman's features. "Did Amy have you listed as the next of kin on her leasing application?"

"I'm not sure," Grace admitted. "I've only lived here in Houston a few weeks." She paused. "You see, the problem is, I have to choose something for them to…for Amy to…wear."

Understanding dawned in the woman's face. Pity

deepened in her eyes. She reached inside her drawer and withdrew a key. "This is a master. I'll have to let you in myself. I can't just give you the key."

"I understand," Grace said. "And that's fine. I appreciate your help."

The woman got up and they started for the door. "I can't tell you how sorry I am. Amy was a good tenant. Always on time with her rent. Except for that one incident, there was never any trouble with her."

Grace paused with her hand on the door knob. "What incident are you talking about?"

The woman bit her lip, as if worrying about how much to tell the dead woman's sister. "There was a man, Amy's boyfriend, I guess. I gather he was... married." Her gaze flashed to Grace's face. Seeing no signs of resentment, she continued. "He was at her apartment one night when his wife showed up. I live here in the complex, you know. Right across the parking lot from Amy's apartment. Anyway, the woman created such a disturbance I finally had to call the police."

"What did she do?"

Another pause. The woman's frown deepened. "She had a gun. She shot out the tires on her husband's Porsche, and then threatened to use the gun on Amy."

AMY'S APARTMENT WAS decorated in soothing pastels—green, peach and cream. The colors reminded Grace of warm breezes and flower-scented afternoons. Of youth and innocence and everything she'd lost one cold Saturday night.

The apartments Grace had occupied since that night fourteen years ago, when she'd lost her whole family, were places where she slept and sometimes ate. They were never home. Not like this.

For the first time since she'd heard about Amy's death, Grace let herself feel the impact of the loss. She hadn't known Amy well. They'd spoken on only two occasions, once here in Amy's apartment. But Grace had sensed something about the young woman, a loneliness that had touched a chord deep within Grace's own darkness.

The door to Amy's apartment opened, and Grace turned. Ethan stepped tentatively inside. "All right if I come in now?"

Nodding, she motioned him in.

Ethan walked into the room, looking around. "Nice place," he murmured.

"Do you recognize it?"

He glanced at her. "Why? Have I been here before?"

Grace started to tell him the story the manager had related to her, but then decided he'd had enough blows for one day. "I thought you might have, considering."

He walked over to a pine bookshelf and picked up a picture, studying it intently.

Grace knew the picture. Amy had told her about it the night they'd first met, when Grace had come here to talk about Ethan. The photograph was of Amy and a boyfriend who had long since gone his own way, but Amy had told Grace that she liked the way the two of them looked together so she'd kept the picture on display. Grace could see why. Blond and fair, dressed all in white, Amy looked radiant, almost ethereal against a snowy Rocky Mountain backdrop.

Grace walked over and stood beside Ethan. "That's Amy," she said softly. Her eyes were drawn to the picture, and for the first time, she detected a similarity between Amy and Pilar Hunter. The resemblance was not so much in their faces but in the perfection of their features.

"Evidently you have a thing for beautiful women," she said.

Ethan glanced up, his eyes locking with hers. "Evidently, I do."

His gaze dropped almost imperceptibly, touching the curves of Grace's body only briefly before lifting to her face. Something dark flickered in his eyes. Something that made Grace's heart pound in awareness.

For a long moment, neither of them said anything, but the attraction between them was electric.

This can't be happening, Grace thought. *Not here. Not now. And especially not with this man.*

She had a job to do. A killer to find. Nothing could get in her way.

And yet, something *was* getting in her way. Clouding her judgment. Threatening her whole way of life.

She knew that he was going to kiss her, but Grace was powerless to stop it. Powerless to fight it. Powerless to do anything more than close her eyes briefly before his lips touched hers.

And it was only a touch. Nothing more than a faint skimming of their lips, but Grace's heart pounded an erratic rhythm inside her breast. When she made no move to resist, he deepened the kiss, almost urgently, and finally Grace heard the warnings that were screaming inside her head. *You can't do this! You're risking everything!*

Besides which, he was a married man.

Immediately, Grace stepped back, glaring at him angrily, trying to convince herself she'd had no part in the kiss. Trying to reassure herself it would never, ever happen again.

She waited for the platitudes and the apologies. The *I'm sorry. It was a mistake. I don't know what came over me* excuse.

Instead he stared down at her, his dark eyes openly defiant, as if he were daring her to deny the blatant sexual chemistry between them.

Without a word, Grace turned and walked out of the room.

Chapter Six

Inside Amy's bedroom, Grace stood leaning against the wall, eyes closed, while she tried to get her heartbeat, her emotions, under control.

What would Myra say if she could see her protégée now—pulse pounding, hands trembling, stomach fluttering like a schoolgirl's? This was so unlike Grace. She never lost control.

She opened her eyes and took several long breaths. All right, so the kiss had been a mistake. No question about that, but there was nothing to be done but put it behind her. Stop thinking about it and get back to work.

Grace knew all about using work to forget. There had been times when her job was all that had kept her going. After all she'd been through, a kiss seemed so inconsequential.

And yet...

It hadn't been just a kiss. That was the problem. It had been an acknowledgment of the attraction— the dangerous kind—that existed between her and Ethan Hunter. The kind of attraction that made people forget who and what they were, and why they shouldn't be together.

But that can't happen, Grace told herself firmly. *It*

won't happen. After all the years of indifference—of *celibacy,* for God's sake—it would take more than a man without a memory, a man with a dangerous past, to awaken her sleeping libido.

Grace would make sure of it.

She drew another long breath and glanced around. She knew it was pointless to search Amy's bedroom. Anything helpful or incriminating would have already been removed. So instead, she opened the closet and glanced through Amy's beautiful clothing, selecting a simple black knit dress and a pair of black heels. Opening the jewelry box on Amy's dresser, Grace removed a string of pearls and a pair of matching earrings.

Just as she closed the jewelry box lid, she heard voices from the other room. Grace thought at first Ethan had turned on the stereo or TV, but when she walked to the bedroom door, she saw a man in a powder-blue suit talking with Ethan.

Grace had never met the man, but she knew who he was. As she entered the room, both pairs of males eyes turned on her, and a shiver of apprehension slipped up her spine.

Ethan introduced her to Sergeant Pope with the Houston Police Department, and the detective lifted his grizzled eyebrows as he took her in. "You were at the crime scene last night. I didn't meet you myself, but Webber told me about you. He said you were pretty distraught. Only natural, I guess, considering."

"Yes, Sergeant Webber was very courteous under the circumstances," Grace said. "I appreciated that."

"Refresh my memory," Pope said. "I don't seem to remember what you were doing at the clinic last night."

Grace glanced at Ethan. He was staring at her curiously. Maybe even a little suspiciously, and no wonder. She'd failed to mention to him that she'd been at the crime scene just minutes after he and Amy had been taken away. Any hint of the passion she'd glimpsed in his eyes earlier had vanished.

She turned back to Pope. "Amy and I were supposed to have dinner. She called and said she might be running a little late because she was going by the clinic first. I went to the restaurant and waited for her, but after a while, I got worried. The clinic isn't in the safest area of town, you know, so I decided to go by and check on her." Grace paused, her gaze dropping to the black dress draped across her arm and the pearls and shoes clutched in her hands. "The police were already there when I arrived." Her gaze lifted to Ethan's. "Dr. Hunter and Amy had already been taken away."

"That's what you meant last night when you said the police had talked to you?" Ethan asked.

She nodded. "They told me what had happened, and then Sergeant Webber asked me to go down to the morgue with him and identify Amy's body." Grace shuddered, remembering the coldness of the room, the steel vaults. The dead bodies. She would never get used to that. Never.

The detective glanced at first Grace, then Ethan. "How did the two of you hook up?"

Before Ethan had a chance to answer, Grace said, "I went by the hospital to see how he was doing. When I learned he was checking himself out, I volunteered to drive him home. And then knowing how difficult it would be, he offered to come over here with me today. I thought it was...very considerate."

The suspicion in Ethan's eyes turned to puzzlement.

Who are you? his expression seemed to be saying. *What the hell do you think you're doing?*

"I hope we haven't done anything wrong, Sergeant." Grace widened her eyes innocently. "Letting ourselves in here, I mean. There wasn't any crime scene tape on the door, or anything."

Pope's gaze narrowed on her. "How *did* you get in? You have a key?"

"The apartment manager let us in. I explained that I needed to get some of Amy's clothes for her to be...buried in. The funeral is tomorrow."

The detective looked surprised. "Tomorrow? That's rushing it a little, isn't it?"

"Not really." Grace shrugged. "Amy and I don't have any family, no out-of-town relatives to wait for. I just want to get it over with as soon as possible. There won't be a problem...getting her body released, will there?"

Again Grace felt Ethan's gaze on her, but this time she kept her attention on Pope. His awful blue suit, greased hair and world-weary expression didn't fool her one bit. He was sharp. As soon as he got back to the station, he would check out her story. Grace had no doubt about that.

"Shouldn't be a problem," he said. "The coroner has already filed his report. Didn't take long to figure out the cause of death." When Grace winced, he said, "Sorry. Sometimes you forget."

He took a few steps into the room, gazing around. With his back still turned to them, he said, "So why did you check yourself out of the hospital, Dr. Hunter? You were in pretty bad shape when I left you last night."

Ethan exchanged a glance with Grace, one that said, *We're going to talk about all this later. Trust me.*

"I wanted to get home, rest in my own bed. I don't like hospitals."

Pope turned at that. "Worrisome hang-up for a doctor, wouldn't you say?"

"Not at all," Ethan said smoothly. "I think you'll find most of my colleagues have that same 'hang-up.' You've heard the expression Doctors Make The Worst Patients. I'm afraid it's true."

He was good, Grace thought. Quick on his feet. Almost frighteningly so. She stared at him with new admiration.

"I came by to see you this morning," Pope said. He withdrew a wallet and a passport from the inside pocket of his suit coat. He handed the items to Ethan. "I wanted to give you these. I'll have someone deliver the luggage and your briefcase to your house later today."

Ethan gazed at the wallet and passport for several seconds before putting them away in his own jacket pocket. Grace could only guess what he was thinking. A wallet meant information. A passport could mean freedom.

The detective finished his perusal of the room and turned back to them. He nodded to the clothing in Grace's arms. "Looks like you got what you came for. The mortuary you select will take care of the arrangements with the morgue."

"Thank you." Grace turned to Ethan. "I guess we should be going then. I still have other arrangements to make."

"Right."

They headed for the door, but Pope made no move

to follow them. "I'll lock up when I leave," he said pointedly.

They left him standing in the center of the room, studying Amy's apartment with a keenness, an intensity that Grace found particularly unnerving. She hoped to hell he didn't stumble across something one of Myra's operatives might have missed.

OUTSIDE, ETHAN TOOK her arm when she started down the sidewalk toward the parking lot. "Not so fast," he said. "I want to know what was going on back there."

Grace glanced up at him. "What do you mean?"

"For starters, I'd like to know why you didn't tell me about your being at the clinic last night. You led me to believe the police had called you to tell you about Amy."

"No, I didn't," Grace argued. "All I said was that I'd talked to the police. And I did. What difference does it make if I was at the clinic or at home?"

"What were you doing at the clinic?" Ethan's hand was still on her arm. His grip wasn't tight, but Grace knew that if she tried to walk away, he would hold her. He had too many questions right now to let her go.

"Just what I said. Amy and I were supposed to meet. When she didn't show up, I got worried so I went to the clinic looking for her." Grace knew her words were convincing, but she wasn't as certain about her expression. She slipped on her sunglasses, not wanting to reveal too much.

After a moment, he said, "Why didn't you tell me about Amy's funeral?"

"You didn't ask." When he started to protest, she interrupted coolly, "You didn't ask, so I figured you didn't care. Amy didn't mean anything to you."

His gaze darkened as he stared down at her. "How do you know that?"

"Because you wouldn't have kissed me if she had." There, Grace thought. She'd brought up the kiss deliberately so they could get it out in the open, so that she could make her feelings for him very, very clear. She glanced down at his hand on her arm, arched a brow over her sunglasses, and he released her.

"Then you must not have cared about her either," he said.

"How dare you say that to me? She was my sister."

Ethan's gaze darkened. "Are you denying that you kissed me back?"

"I didn't." Grace was surprised to find that her outrage was more instinctive than studied. She wasn't sure she quite understood it.

"We kissed," he said, glaring down at her. "It was a mutual action. And just because I'm not denying it doesn't mean I'm exactly proud of what's happening between us."

Grace hadn't expected that. She stared at him uncertainly. "What do you mean?"

"I'm a married man, Grace."

It was like a slap in the face. Not that Grace had forgotten his marital status. Far from it. But in truth, that was only one of many reasons why she couldn't allow herself to become involved with Ethan Hunter. She supposed she should be glad that he'd suddenly developed scruples.

"All right," she said calmly. "We both agree that it was a mistake. It won't happen again. There's no reason why it should have to affect our working relationship. We're both adults."

Something glinted in his eyes. "You think it'll be that easy?"

"Yes," she said simply. "Because it has to be."

After a moment, he said, "All right. We'll forget about the kiss. We'll pretend it never happened. We'll promise ourselves it won't happen again, but there's something else we need to get straight."

"What?"

His gaze held hers. "I may not have my memory, but I'm not as stupid or as helpless as you seem to think. I don't know why you won't go to the police with what you know, but I'm pretty sure it has nothing to do with Amy."

Grace was glad her eyes were hidden behind the dark glasses. "I don't know what you're talking about. I already explained why I don't want to involve the police."

"Because you don't want to ruin Amy's good name. Because to the police she's just another statistic. It doesn't wash, Grace."

Her heart started to pound, whether from his accusations or from the way he said her name, Grace wasn't sure.

He didn't touch her again, but she couldn't have moved if her life depended on it.

His eyes narrowed suspiciously. "You're talking about catching a cold-blooded murderer. An assassin, you said. It takes a little more than guts to do that."

"I know that," she said almost angrily. "I'm not as stupid or as helpless as *you* seem to think."

"Oh, I don't think you're stupid or helpless." His gaze deepened on her. "Far from it. I think you're very, very clever."

"Don't give me too much credit," she muttered. Because this conversation certainly wasn't going the way she'd anticipated.

"You're not telling me everything," he accused. "Don't think I don't know it."

"I would never make the mistake of underestimating you," Grace said truthfully. Especially not now. "But I've told you everything I know. I've tried to make you understand why this is so important to me. Don't you see? If I had shown up at the clinic a few minutes earlier last night, Amy would still be alive. If I hadn't turned my back on her years ago, she never would have moved to Houston in the first place. She never would have gotten involved with...you. I've always let her down, and now she's dead because of me." Grace paused, feeling the old horror rise up inside her as the memories came swarming back. It had taken her a long time to beat back the monsters, to subdue the night terrors that had once threatened her sanity. Amy's death, and the man who had killed her, had brought it all back.

"How can I live with myself if I let her killer go free?" Grace whispered.

Ethan couldn't see her eyes, and Grace thought fleetingly that perhaps she should remove her sunglasses and let him witness the anguish, the sudden tears that were almost as foreign to her as the attraction she felt for him. She wasn't opposed to using her emotions to get what she needed, but this was too much. Too... intense.

"I can tell you've been hurt," Ethan said softly. "When you drift off like that, I can tell you're experiencing grief. But I'm not sure the grief is for Amy."

When Grace said nothing, he took a step toward her, towering over her like a menacing embodiment of her conscience. "I don't know what's going on here," he said. "I don't know what part I played in Amy's death, or why you seem so willing to work with a man you have every reason to despise. But I do know this." He removed her dark glasses, then put a gentle finger beneath her chin and tilted her head back so that he could stare down into her eyes. "Attraction or not, God help you if you're lying to me."

GRACE LET HERSELF into her room that night and reached for the light switch. Her hand froze before she made the connection. Something was different about the room. She could detect a subtle scent that didn't belong there.

Standing motionless, Grace listened to the dark. Then very quietly, she slipped her hand inside her purse and withdrew her gun, releasing the safety as her gaze searched the darkness. A breeze touched her face, and she realized suddenly that the sliding glass door was open. She started across the room toward it just as a voice said from the balcony, "It's only me, Grace. Put away your gun."

Grace let the weapon drop to her side, but she didn't put it away as she stepped out on the balcony to join Myra Temple. The woman sat in darkness, the only substance to her shadowy form the arcing glow of her cigarette as she lifted it to her mouth. In the silence that followed, Grace could hear the tiny crackle as the flames ate away at the paper holding the tobacco.

"How did it go today?" Myra asked. Her voice, husky from years of smoking, was one men dreamed of.

Grace replaced the gun in her purse before answering. "I think he'll cooperate."

"How much did you tell him?"

"Almost everything. The truth is almost always more convincing than lies. I've heard you say that dozens of times."

The cigarette lifted again. "He still thinks you're Amy's sister, though. You didn't tell him the truth about that."

"No." Because a man who had managed to stay one step ahead of the law wasn't likely to throw in his lot with an FBI agent. Not a man as resourceful and wealthy as Ethan Hunter.

She thought about their last conversation, the threat he'd given her, and in spite of the heat, Grace shivered. "You have someone watching the house tonight?" she asked.

"Huddleston and Smith have the first watch, but they'll be relieved after midnight, just like last night."

Grace nodded, satisfied. She wondered suddenly what Ethan was doing all alone in that house. Or was he alone? Had Pilar decided to pay him another visit?

Against her will, Grace conjured up an image of Ethan's wife—the lithe body, the glossy hair, the incredible face. What a handsome couple they would make. In her mind's eye, Grace could see the two of them together, in each other's arms. Naked. Kissing. Making love.

She thought about the way Ethan had looked at her today in Amy's apartment, the brief kiss they had shared, and the image changed. She could see herself in his arms. Naked. Kissing. Making love.

I'm a married man, Grace.

"So what are you doing sitting out here in the dark?" she asked Myra, trying to dispel the forbidden image in her mind.

She sensed rather than saw Myra's shrug. "Strangely enough, I've been thinking about the past."

"Don't tell me you're getting maudlin." Grace sank into the green plastic lawn chair next to Myra's. "You always told me the past is a dangerous pitfall, one that should be avoided at all costs."

Grace heard the tinkle of ice against glass as Myra lifted a drink to her lips. "I know, but lately it's become harder and harder for me to avoid that particular pitfall. I find myself reflecting at the oddest times. I guess it comes with age."

"No way," Grace said. "You're still a young woman." Still vibrant and beautiful, though there'd been times when Grace could have sworn her mentor ate nails for breakfast. Grace wasn't the only one in the Bureau who had thought so. Myra Temple was almost legendary.

Myra sighed, an uncharacteristic sound for her. "I may not be old in the real world, but forty-three can be ancient in our world, Grace."

She had a point. Grace fell silent for a moment, contemplating her own life. In twelve years, she would be Myra's age. Would she then *want* to look back, to reflect as Myra had put it? Somehow Grace couldn't imagine it.

Myra picked up a tiny whiskey bottle—the kind stocked in the room bar—from beside her chair and set it on the plastic table between them. The seal on the bottle was broken, but Grace knew Myra's own drink contained no alcohol. She was very disciplined in that regard. The empty bottle was to make a point.

"All right, so I had one drink last night," Grace admitted, wishing she didn't sound so defensive. Wishing she didn't have a reason to be. "But that's all. It won't happen again. You can take the bar key with you if it makes you feel any better.''

Myra tossed her cigarette butt over the balcony to the asphalt parking lot below them. Tiny sparks rained down in the darkness. "That won't be necessary. I know you remember how bad it was for you back then. But you're strong now, Grace. Stronger than me in a lot of ways.''

Grace didn't think that was possible. Myra was unparalleled. She would never consider drinking alone in the middle of the night, much less making love to a man whose secrets just might be even darker than her own.

"Do you remember the first time we met?" Myra asked suddenly. "You were only seventeen, but I sensed that resilience in you even then. I hated the fact that your father always seemed hell-bent on breaking you.''

Don't, Grace thought. *Don't take me back there.*

She closed her eyes, letting the hot breeze blow across her face, willing away the melancholy that seemed to have gripped both her and Myra.

Beside her, Myra shifted restlessly in her chair. "You came by the office to see your father that day. He'd just learned I was to be his new partner. He wasn't too pleased to discover I was a woman.''

"Some things never change," Grace said. "The Bureau is still a man's world.''

"True enough," Myra said. "But you're becoming a damned fine agent, Grace. You've earned a lot of respect.''

"So have you. You paved the way for women like me. I'll always be grateful.'' For that and so much more, but Grace left the words unspoken. Over the years, she and Myra had developed an internal method of communicating. They'd been through a lot together, but Grace couldn't help wondering if this was to be their final assignment. When Trevor Reardon was no longer their nemesis, who or what would then become their raison d'être?

Myra stood and stretched. "By the way, we lifted some fresh prints from Hunter's clinic last night after the police left. I'll let you know as soon as I hear back from the lab."

Grace got up and walked her to the door. In the light from the corridor, Myra suddenly looked much older than her years. It made Grace uneasy, watching her.

Grace remained at the door until the agent disappeared around a corner. After a moment, Grace heard the ping of the elevator and the sound of the doors sliding open and then shut again. Only then did she close and lock her door. But she didn't turn on the light. She stood in the darkness as the memories came flooding back.

Putting her hands to her ears, she tried to shut them out, but Myra's pensiveness tonight had inadvertently opened a Pandora's box. In her mind, Grace saw the house where she'd grown up bursting into flames. She heard her mother's terrified cries, her father's anguished shouts, and her sister's tormented screams.

Grace closed her eyes, trembling. It had taken her years to get those images out of her head. Years of therapy and cold indifference before she no longer saw her sister, her hair in flames, at every window. Years of single-minded devotion to her career to block out the argument she and Jessica had had just hours before her sister's death.

Like a roller-coaster out of control, Grace's mind

whipped around the perilous corners of her past, plunged downward into the murky depths of her memory. Faces flew past her. Scenes blurred by her. She wished she could stop them—she would do anything to stop them—but it was too late for that. Too late to do anything but huddle in the darkness and remember.

There had been a man. Grace had sensed from the first that he was different, someone special, but she hadn't learned until later just how extraordinary he was. When she'd first met him at the library during the Christmas break of her senior year in high school, all she'd known was that he was a dashing older man, probably at least thirty, and more sophisticated and worldly than she could ever have imagined.

She'd also thought that he was the most handsome man she'd ever seen. When he looked up from the book he was reading and smiled at her, Grace knew instantly he was the one. The two of them had a connection, some special bond that had drawn her to him. His eyes were blue, his hair golden brown, and even in the dead of winter, he was suntanned, as if he'd just come from the slopes of some exotic ski resort.

Grace grew so nervous, just watching him, that she dropped the book she was holding. His smile broadened, as if he knew he was the source of her anxiety and was pleased by the knowledge. Grace turned and all but ran from the room.

The next day, she saw him again at the library. This time, her nerves in check, she took a seat two tables away from his, facing him. Every time she looked up from her book, she found his gaze on her, and Grace's insides quivered in delicious anticipation.

On the third day, he approached her. He stood over her table, hands planted on the surface as he bent down to whisper in her ear. Grace could smell the intoxicating scent of his cologne, could see the faint shadow of his beard, and her heart went wild. This was no boy, but a *man.*

"Do you want to get out of here?" he whispered, his voice deep and knowing.

Grace could only nod. He removed the book from her hands, then pulled her to her feet. Clasping her hand in his, he led her outside to the parking area, to an expensive sports car that made Grace catch her breath.

"This is your car?"

He dangled the keys before her. "Would you like to drive it?"

Grace had her license but her father rarely let her behind the wheel of the family sedan. His career in the FBI had made him overly protective of his family, and Grace's nature had made her openly rebellious. The two of them often clashed. She wondered fleetingly what her father would think if he could see her now.

In spite of her defiant nature, the image subdued Grace a little. This man was a total stranger after all. She shook her head. "I'd better not."

"Oh, come on," he said in that dark and silky voice. "You know you want to. For once in your life, live dangerously."

The challenge was irresistible. Grace took the keys from his fingers, and he opened the door for her. So gallant and so unlike the boys she'd dated. She slid behind the wheel and waited until he climbed into the passenger side before starting the car.

The engine roared to life, the sound thrumming through Grace's veins like a shot of pure adrenaline. So this was power, she thought.

The man put his hand over hers on the stick shift, helping her find the right gear. His touch made her shiver. Grace glanced at him warily. "Where are we going?"

"Anywhere you want to go, Grace."

That stopped her for a minute. Her excitement cooled. "How do you know my name?"

He smiled, pulling a card from his pocket and holding it up to her. It was her library card. "You dropped it that first day," he said, "When you were running away from me."

"I wasn't running away from you," Grace protested, not wanting him to think of her as a child.

"Maybe you should have." His smile turned mysterious. "I'm a dangerous man, Grace."

"I know."

Their gazes met and held for the longest moment, then he reached over and grasped the back of her neck, pulling her toward him. His mouth found hers and almost instantly, Grace felt his tongue plunge inside.

She knew she should pull away. This man was way too old and way too experienced for her, and he was a stranger. A stranger who kissed her like no boy had ever kissed her. Who made her feel the way no one had ever made her feel. Who whispered to her things no one had ever told her.

"You're very beautiful," he murmured. "You have no idea how special you are to me, Grace."

Something warm unfurled inside her, some womanly need that made her cling to him, that made her groan against his mouth, that made her want him in ways she'd hardly dared dream about.

She drove them to his apartment a few blocks from where she lived, and they talked a little, trying to get to know one another, trying to ease the almost unbearable tension between them. But all the while they both knew the inevitable would happen—*had* to happen—before she left him that night.

They met again the next night, and the next. Grace was barely allowed to date boys her own age, so she knew bringing him home to meet her parents, especially her father, was out of the question. She started sneaking out of her room at night, begging her younger sister, Jessie, to cover for her.

Unlike Grace, Jessie had never been rebellious. She had always worked very hard to please their father, and lying to him went against her nature. Grace understood that, but her sister's conscience didn't matter enough to Grace to make her want to stop seeing *him*.

On the night of the fire, Jessie had been especially troubled by Grace's deception. She even threatened to tell their parents and take her own punishment for the duplicity if Grace left the house again without their permission.

Grace lashed out at her, calling her a Goody Two-shoes. "Why don't you mind your own business for once," she snapped before climbing out the window and slipping away into the darkness to meet her lover.

That night, he seemed different. Before, he'd always been dark and intense, even moody at times, but Grace had found those qualities deeply compelling. Tonight, however, he was almost ebullient, laughing and smiling, whispering to her that he had a secret.

It was only…afterward that Grace learned what his secret was.

"Would you like to know my real name?" he asked, drawing her fingers to his lips and kissing each one of them.

Grace gazed up at him in confusion. "Your name is Jonathan Price."

He laughed out loud. "Jonathan Price is a fictional character, you little idiot. I got it from a novel."

Grace didn't much care for the insult. She pulled away from him.

He didn't even seem to notice. "I go by many names, but the one you may have heard of is Trevor Reardon."

He laughed again when he saw the horror dawn on her face.

"That isn't funny," she said, shaken. Nothing about him was the least bit amusing. In fact, he was beginning to scare her. Grace jumped up, pulling on her clothes while he lay on the bed, smiling that taunting little smile. "Trevor Reardon is in prison," she said.

"So you have heard of me." He propped himself on his elbow. "I didn't think your old man could resist bragging about the coup he pulled off when he captured me. But didn't he also tell you that I'd escaped from prison a few weeks ago? Didn't he warn you I might come back for revenge?"

Her father *had* been acting strangely lately, even more protective than usual, making the whole family promise to be home by dark every day. Maybe that's why Jessie had been so frightened when Grace had started sneaking out of the house at night. Maybe she'd known something Grace hadn't.

Dressed by this time, Grace started backing toward the door. She didn't believe him, *couldn't* believe him, and yet...

What if he was telling her the truth?

What if he was Trevor Reardon?

She put a hand to her mouth, trying to swallow back

a rising tide of nausea. "Who are you?" she whispered. "Why are you doing this to me?"

"It's all been a game," he said. "And you've been so much fun." He got out of bed and stood naked before her. "But playtime's over, Grace. It's time to get to work."

Her hand on the door knob, she said weakly, "If I scream someone will hear me. The police will come."

"Oh, I wouldn't wait for the police if I were you. Your family may need you, even as we speak."

She saw the truth in his eyes. Knew that he had done something unspeakable to her family while she lay in his arms.

Grace turned and fled the apartment. He didn't try to follow her, but she could hear his laughter echoing in the darkness all around her.

Five blocks away from her house, she heard the sirens. Two blocks away, she saw the flames. When she reached the driveway, she heard the screams.

Oh, God, oh, God, oh, God, was all she could think as she rushed toward the burning house. Someone grabbed her and held her back. She struggled to free herself, and it was then that she looked up and saw Jessie at their bedroom window. Sweet little Jessie pounding at the double panes, screaming in terror and agony as her clothing and hair caught fire.

And somewhere in the darkness, Grace could hear Trevor Reardon, still laughing....

As the memories all but consumed her, Grace slumped against the wall of her hotel room, weak and dizzy. Even after all these years, the thought of his mouth on her, his hands touching her sent her flying to the bathroom. She lay spent and trembling on the floor moments later, the memories still closing in on her like a crushing weight. She willed them away, but they resisted. They weren't through with her yet. There was still more to be endured, other horrors to relive.

Groaning, Grace rolled to her side, feeling the cool tile against her cheek.

After that night, the guilt and grief over her family's deaths had almost killed her, but Trevor Reardon hadn't been finished with her. Dressed as one of the cops standing guard at the church, he attended the funeral service for her family three days later. Grace knew this because he called her afterward and described in detail the clothing she'd had on, right down to the tiny pearls she'd worn in her ears.

The knowledge that he had been that close to her again very nearly drove Grace over the edge. If it hadn't been for Myra Temple, Grace wasn't sure she would have survived.

But Myra helped her through the worst of those days. She forced Grace from the pit of despair she'd crawled into. Made her stop drinking. Made her realize that Reardon would win again if Grace let him.

So with Myra's help, Grace went on to college and eventually graduated from law school. After a while, she could even pretend she led a normal life. At times, she even managed to forget that a killer was out there somewhere, still waiting for her.

But Myra never forgot.

On the night Grace graduated from law school, Reardon was waiting for her in her apartment. He grabbed her, threw her on her bed, and, knife to her throat, told her exactly what he was going to do to her.

But then Myra came bursting into Grace's bedroom, and the agents with her had quickly subdued Reardon. Myra calmly walked over to him, and with a hand that was completely steady, put a gun to his head. For a moment, Grace thought she would pull the trigger. Wanted her to pull the trigger.

But then Myra lowered the weapon, Reardon was taken away, and Grace collapsed in the agent's arms. Grace promised herself that the tears she shed that night would be her last. That she would never again allow herself to be vulnerable. To be a target.

Within a month, she made the life-altering decision to follow in her father's footsteps at the FBI. When she was accepted so quickly, she suspected that Myra had pulled some strings, but Grace didn't care. She was completely focused. She knew exactly what she wanted from life. While Trevor Reardon was confined to a maximum security prison some seven hundred miles away, Grace began and completed the rigorous training at Quantico, Virginia.

She became an agent as dedicated and single-minded as any who had served before her. If she was lonely at night, she tried not to think about it. If she had difficulty making friends, she told herself she didn't have time for relationships anyway. If she shied away from serious involvements, she knew that was the way it had to be. There was no room in her life for anything but justice.

For Grace, her emotional isolation had become a normal way of life.

But then three months ago, news had come to her of Trevor Reardon's second escape. She hadn't been surprised. Or frightened. In fact, there had been a certain sense of inevitability about it all. She'd always known he would come back for her. She was the one loose end that would torment him.

But it would be different now, Grace thought, lying

in the bright glare of the bathroom light. This time, she would be ready for him. This time, she was the hunter.

And when they met again face to face, she and Reardon, this time, only one of them would walk away.

Chapter Seven

The aroma of frying chorizo awakened Ethan the next morning. He sat up in bed, wondering at his ability to identify the scent of the spicy Mexican sausage when he still had no recall of his past life.

The enticing smell drew a rumble from his stomach, reminding him that he'd skipped dinner the previous evening. He got up from bed and hurriedly showered and shaved. Staring at himself in the mirror, he noticed that the bruises were fading, the swelling had gone away, and the cut was starting to heal.

He studied his features dispassionately. Ethan supposed his appearance would be considered above average by most standards, but to him, there was still something disturbing about his face. Something that wasn't quite right.

Not wanting to dwell on the possibilities, he left the bathroom and hurriedly dressed, letting the spicy aroma lead him downstairs and into the kitchen.

Rosa stood at the range, stirring the cooked chorizo into a batch of fluffy scrambled eggs. She turned when she heard Ethan enter the room.

"*Buenos días,* Dr. Hunter." She gave him a critical

once-over. "You're looking much better this morning."

"Thanks. I feel better." He walked over to the breakfast table and sat down at the place she had set for him.

"I made your favorite today. Chorizo and eggs."

"Smells great." Ethan watched as she dished up a plate of the sausage and eggs, then brought it to him. She waited while he sampled a bite, then beamed when he almost choked on the peppery food.

"A little extra Tabasco sauce this morning," she explained. "It'll get your blood flowing, speed up your recovery."

Ethan's blood was flowing all right. He felt as if it were about to explode out the top of his head. "Do you think I could have a glass of orange juice?" he managed to gasp.

Rosa stood with her hands on her hips, watching him. "Since when do you like orange juice?"

"Since I found a pitcher in the refrigerator yesterday."

"That was for me," Rosa said accusingly. "You don't like orange juice, not even fresh squeezed. You drink *jugo de tomate*."

Tomato juice didn't sound the least bit appealing to Ethan, but if it would put out the flames dancing on his tongue, he was willing to give it a shot.

"All right, tomato juice then."

Rosa still hesitated. "That cut on your head, Dr. Hunter. It still makes you strange, no?"

"Strange is a good word for it," he muttered.

Rosa turned and hurried over to the refrigerator. She brought him back a tall glass of chilled tomato juice.

Ethan took a quick drink, then another. It wasn't half bad.

He set down the glass and glanced up at Rosa. "You were right. *Jugo de tomate* hits the spot."

She nodded in satisfaction, then circled the air with her finger near her ear. *"Extraño."* She started to turn away, then stopped. She stared down at him, her dark eyes clouding. "I read in the paper about Amy Cole. Dr. Hunter, why didn't you tell me what had happened to you the other night?"

"I didn't want to worry you, Rosa."

She bit her lip, twisting her hands in her white apron. "That poor child. I only met her once, when she came here to the house looking for you, but she was very nice to me."

Ethan nodded, not wanting to encourage a line of conversation to which he had nothing to contribute. He didn't remember Amy. He didn't remember anything about her, only the sound of her scream before she'd died.

He glanced down at his plate, willing away the image.

Rosa must have mistaken his silence for grief. She murmured something comforting in Spanish, then turned and went back to her work.

Ethan took a few more bites of his food, then shoved his plate away. At the thought of Amy, his appetite had deserted him. After several minutes of strained silence, he said, "By the way, how's your daughter and her baby?"

Rosa turned at that, her look one of astonishment.

"What's the matter?" Ethan asked in alarm. "Did I say something wrong?"

Rosa's amazement turned to discomfort. Her dark

brows knitted into a frown. "No. It's just that…why do you want to know about my daughter, Dr. Hunter? It's been a long time since you ask about her."

"It…has?"

Rosa hesitated. "We don't talk about our personal lives to each other. That was the agreement we had when I first came to work for you. You said it would be better that way."

"Better for whom?"

Her shrug seemed ominous somehow. She came back over to the table and stood staring down at him. "Dr. Hunter, are you sure you're okay? Maybe you should go back to the hospital." She pronounced it "ohs-pee-tahl."

"Don't worry about me." Ethan tried to shrug away her concern. "I told you it might take several days for the effects of the concussion to wear off."

"I know, but it's not just that." Rosa paused again. "You don't act the same. You don't talk the same. You don't even look the same…" She trailed off, one hand creeping to her chest as if she had the sudden urge to cross herself.

Ethan frowned. "I still have a lot of bruising on my face, and my voice is still a bit hoarse." He wondered why his tone suddenly sounded so defensive.

"Maybe," Rosa agreed, but she didn't look convinced. "I still think you should go back to the hospital."

Ethan tried to smile reassuringly. "Just give me a few more days. I'll be back up to speed in no time."

Rosa muttered something he couldn't understand as she turned back to the stove.

Ethan got up and carried his plate and glass to the

sink. "Do we have a phone book around here somewhere?"

"In the cabinet next to the door," she said, watching him. Ethan thought she was probably dying to ask him who he wanted to call. In spite of the agreement about their private lives, he could see the curiosity—or was that suspicion?—simmering in the black depths of her eyes.

He retrieved the Yellow Pages directory from the shelf, and carried the two heavy volumes back to his place at the table. Thumbing through the A-L volume, he located the page he wanted, then quickly scanned the entries underneath Guns. He memorized the name and address of a store on the Katy Freeway that looked promising, but he had no idea how to find it. All he knew was that his house was somewhere off Memorial Drive.

Checking the map at the front of the book, he discovered that the Katy Freeway was the name of the feeder road that ran alongside Interstate 10, and that the gun shop was not far from where he lived. He was fairly certain he could find it.

Closing the book, he put both volumes back in their places and turned to Rosa. Her expression was still dubious.

If you only knew the whole story, Ethan thought. Aloud, he said, "Do you happen to know where my car keys are?"

"No. But I know where you keep your spares." She opened a drawer, pulled out a key, and tossed it to him. Ethan decided the Porsche emblem on the key ring was a good omen.

He pocketed the key. "By the way, I think it would be a good idea to get the alarm code changed. I'd like for you to contact the security company as soon as possible.''

Following the covered walkway to the garage, Ethan opened the side door and pressed the lighted button on the wall to activate the automatic garage door opener. The heavy door slowly lifted, letting in sunlight, and Ethan, getting his first look at the Porsche, whistled softly.

Black and sleek, with a mirrorlike finish that was almost blinding, the sports car looked ready and able for action. But almost equally impressive was the vintage candy apple–red Corvette that sat alongside the Porsche, and the white 1964 T-Bird that was parked next to the Vette.

Ethan took a moment to admire all three cars before climbing into the Porsche and backing it out of the garage. Shifting into gear, he gave the car gas, then heard the satisfactory burn of rubber as he headed down the driveway.

A Porsche, a Corvette, and a Thunderbird, he thought admiringly. For the first time since he'd awakened in the hospital, he considered the possibilities—and the privileges—that came with being Dr. Ethan Hunter. Maybe there were certain aspects of his personality that he could admire after all. He apparently had fantastic taste in cars.

And in women.

If the picture he'd seen of Amy Cole yesterday was any indication, she'd been as beautiful as his wife, Pilar, but for some reason Ethan couldn't explain, neither woman seemed real to him. They were almost too perfect, as if he had chosen them—or created them—to be admired rather than loved. In spite of their great beauty, both women left him cold.

Ethan supposed he could attribute his lack of an emotional response to his amnesia, but how would that explain the exact opposite reaction he had to Grace? Her imperfections—the cleft in her chin, the freckles across her nose, the tiny mole beneath her right eyebrow—were infinitely more appealing and more seductive than flawless features could ever be.

She was a real woman and she would know real passion. Ethan was sure of it. He'd glimpsed that passion in her eyes yesterday, before he'd kissed her. Before she'd fled Amy's living room in a vain attempt to run away from their attraction.

But the chemistry had still been there when she'd come back. Still there when he'd gazed into her eyes outside the apartment, and later, when she'd dropped him off at his house that evening.

It had still been there when he'd fallen asleep last night, thinking about her...

In the space of two short days, Grace Donovan had gotten under his skin in a way he knew no other woman had before her. But a relationship with her was impossible, for any number of reasons. He had no memory. He had no idea what he might have done in his past. And the one thing that did seem certain was that he was a married man. He may have had an affair with Amy Cole, but he wouldn't do that to Grace.

What about Pilar? a little voice taunted him. *Aren't you the least bit concerned about your wife's feelings?*

Ethan tried, he really tried to feel something for his estranged wife, but nothing came to him. Nothing but an uneasy feeling that Pilar might have been behind his attack two nights ago, that she might have been the one who had wanted Amy dead.

He glanced in the rearview mirror. The streets

weren't crowded this time of day, and Ethan had noticed a white sedan pull out of the neighborhood behind him and trail several car lengths away. But just when Ethan began to think he was being followed, the sedan signalled and turned into the parking area of a large office building.

Just to be on the safe side, Ethan circled the block. When he came back around, the car was still in the parking lot and no one was inside.

A few moments later, Ethan pulled into the shopping center off the Katy Freeway. The gun shop was located between a dry cleaners and a sporting goods store. He parked at the far end of the lot, near the sporting goods store, then removed the unloaded gun from the front seat of the car and slipped it into his jacket pocket.

At this time of morning—a few minutes after ten—stores had just opened. There was no one inside the gun shop except for a clerk who stood behind the counter, polishing the glass. He buzzed Ethan in, and when he entered the store, he could hear another worker in the back, moving inventory.

"Mornin'," the clerk at the counter greeted. He was a tall, lanky man of about fifty, dressed in a white western shirt with pearl buttons and Wrangler jeans that rode low on lean hips. "What can I do you for?"

The store was filled with weapons of varying makes and caliber. Ethan wondered why he didn't feel the least bit intimidated by all that firepower. The thought crossed his mind again that he was no ordinary doctor. Far from it, if what Grace had told him was true.

He stepped up to the counter and pulled the gun from his pocket, laying it carefully on the glass counter. The clerk whistled softly, much as Ethan had done when he'd first seen the Porsche.

"Ain't that a little beauty? What's your askin' price?"

"I'm not here to sell it. I wondered if you could tell me something about it. My father-in-law left it to me when he died," Ethan improvised. "I think it's custom-made."

"Oh, it's custom all right." The clerk picked up the weapon and studied it almost reverently. "It's a 1911 Colt revolver that's been specially modified. See these night sights? Those set your father-in-law back a pretty penny."

Ethan watched the clerk handle the weapon with an expertise that seemed oddly familiar. "Do you have any idea where he might have gotten these modifications?"

The clerk sighted an invisible target, squinting one eye as he took aim. "There's a gun shop over in Arkansas that does this kind of work. They modify weapons of this caliber—guns that can easily be concealed—for police SWAT teams, the FBI Hostage Rescue Units, and even for some of the elite units of the military."

That caught Ethan's attention. "Elite units of the military? You mean like the Navy SEALs?"

The clerk palmed the weapon and tested its weight. "Was your father-in-law a military man?"

"Not in recent years."

"You mean that you know about." The clerk gave him a conspiratorial wink. "Some of those guys are mighty secretive, you know. They don't talk about their work."

Ethan paused. "This gun shop in Arkansas would probably keep records of their custom orders, right?"

The clerk scratched his head. "More than likely. But

if it was ordered through a police department or the military, they wouldn't have a record of the individual the gun was issued to. They might be able to track down the particular law enforcement body or branch of the service that owned the weapon, but I doubt they'd be able to give you that information. And even if they did, it wouldn't do you any good.''

"Why's that?"

"See this?" With his index finger, the clerk traced along the side of the gun barrel. "The identification number has been filed away."

Ethan took the gun from the clerk's hand, holding the weapon to the light. He could barely detect the faint imperfection in the barrel where the number had been removed. Someone had gone to a great deal of trouble to conceal his handiwork. The metal had been polished until the scratches in the finish were all but invisible.

The clerk's eyes narrowed with what might have been suspicion. "Looks like your father-in-law—or someone—wanted to make sure this piece couldn't be traced back to him."

"Well, thanks for your help." Ethan gathered up the weapon, said his goodbye, then hurried out of the shop. He was glad he'd had the foresight to park away from the store. He'd seen the suspicion in the clerk's eyes, and wondered if the man might even now be calling the police. But if he was, he'd have to come outside to get the license plate number from Ethan's car.

Sliding behind the wheel, Ethan quickly started the Porsche and backed out of the space. No one had come out of the gun shop, and he couldn't see anyone at the window. Still, he headed down the street in the wrong direction just to avoid driving by the store.

And all the while, the gun was almost a living, breathing entity in the seat beside him.

He's an ex-Navy SEAL and an explosives expert who sold his services to the highest bidder. He became a mercenary, an assassin, sometimes a terrorist.

Was it possible he had somehow come into possession of Trevor Reardon's weapon? Had Ethan brought it back to the States with him, put it in his safe for—what? Protection? Because he knew Reardon might someday come after him?

Ethan lifted a hand to wipe the sudden beads of sweat from his brow. That had to be it. That had to be the reason he was in possession of such a weapon.

Because the other explanation that came to mind was almost too terrifying to contemplate.

"HE'S NOT HOME?" Grace repeated. "Where did he go?"

The housekeeper shrugged, giving Grace a cool appraisal. "He had errands."

"He didn't give you any indication where he was going?" Damn, Grace thought. Why would he just leave like that? He'd known she was coming over this morning. Why hadn't he waited for her?

And why the hell hadn't someone called her to warn her that he was roaming around out there somewhere, making a target of himself?

Rosa eyed her with open disapproval. "I don't ask where he goes. It's none of my business," she said pointedly.

Grace could tell Rosa didn't like her, and therefore, didn't trust her. Grace had run up against the problem before. She sometimes came across as too abrupt, too impatient, too hard. Women didn't like that. Neither did some men, for that matter.

She forced a softness in her tone. "Look, I don't mean to be such a nuisance, but I need to tell Dr. Hunter about the funeral this afternoon."

"Funeral?"

Grace bit her lip and nodded. "You heard about Amy Cole? Dr. Hunter's assistant?"

Rosa crossed herself. "Yes. Such a shame. So young and so *bella.*"

Grace nodded. "Amy was my sister, Rosa. I came to tell Dr. Hunter about the memorial service this afternoon."

Rosa's expression changed dramatically. The wariness and suspicion vanished, leaving her features set in gentle lines of compassion. "*Lo siento.*" She reached for Grace's hand and pulled her inside. "Please. Come in out of the heat."

She led Grace upstairs, saying over her shoulder, "I'll fix you something cool to drink. Then you can tell me about your sister."

Her soothing tone made Grace want to do exactly that. For the first time in years, she found herself wanting to tell someone about Jessie, about her goodness and purity, and about her unfailing conscience. Jessie had been one of those people who had truly been a blessing to this world, while Grace—

The parrot's harsh squawk brought her abruptly back to the present. She glanced across the room, where the magnificent yellow-and-blue bird strutted with supreme confidence on his perch.

When he saw Grace watching him, he flapped his wings and screeched, "They're not real! They're not real! They're not real!"

"Shut up, Simon, you stupid bird!" Rosa scolded. To Grace she said apologetically, "He's a terrible creature. He picks up everything he hears on the *televisión.*"

Grace wondered which programs he'd been watching. Jerry Springer? Howard Stern, maybe?

She followed Rosa into the kitchen and watched while the housekeeper prepared two glasses of iced tea. They both sat down at the breakfast table—Rosa obviously having dispensed with any formalities—and sipped their drinks.

After a moment, she said, "You came to tell Dr. Hunter about the funeral?"

Grace nodded. "It's at four o'clock this afternoon at the Chapel Hill Funeral Home. I...thought he might like to be there."

Rosa looked as if she wanted to comment but kept silent.

Grace took another sip of her tea. "How long have you worked for Dr. Hunter?"

Rosa shrugged. "A long time."

"You must know him pretty well." Grace studied the older woman's face.

"Dr. Hunter is not an easy man to know. He's very..." Rosa struggled for the right word. "*Complicado.* Complex. There are some who consider him a saint."

"Are you one of them?"

A slight hesitation. "He's no saint. He has his faults, quite a few of them. But he is, in many ways, a very good man."

"You're referring to the work he does at his clinics here and in Mexico."

Rosa nodded. "Especially the one in *Méjico.* The

children who come there would break your heart. Many of them have been horribly disfigured since birth. They've become outcasts in their own villages. They've never known anything but ridicule.''

Grace wondered how he could possibly be the same man who changed criminals faces for money. Was Ethan some sort of Dr. Jekyll and Mr. Hyde, a man with two very distinct personalities? The notion made her shiver. ''How did you meet Dr. Hunter?''

Rosa shrugged, but her expression suddenly became very sad. ''It was a long time ago, in Mexico City. When my daughter was young, I worked in a *barra* in a very bad part of town. Marta and I had a little one-room *apartamento* on the second floor, little better than a hovel, but it was all I could afford. Sometimes when I worked late, Marta would get lonely. She would sneak downstairs to be near me. I didn't want her to. She was already starting to look like a woman, and she was so beautiful that men were already starting to notice her. One night a fight broke out, a drunken brawl. In the confusion, a man grabbed Marta and pulled her outside. He tried to—'' Rosa's eyes closed briefly, as if the memory had become too painful to relive. Grace understood that feeling all too well.

''What happened?'' she asked gently.

Rosa shuddered. ''Marta fought him off as best she could and started screaming. He pulled a knife and cut her. The whole side of her face was…mutilated.''

''I'm sorry.''

Rosa shrugged away Grace's pity. ''She was horribly scarred. People would stare at her on the streets, and children would run away from her. Marta withdrew completely into herself. She was very…ashamed of her face. Years passed, and then one day I heard about Dr.

Hunter. That was before he had his clinic in the jungle. He use to come to Mexico City twice a year and work in one of the hospitals. People there spoke of him as a god. It was said the handsome young doctor could perform miracles, that he could transform the most hideous monster into an angel. Marta was no monster. She was a badly scarred and frightened child. But Dr. Hunter was my only hope.''

"Was he able to help her?" Grace asked, caught up in the story in spite of herself.

"Eventually. Marta was frightened of him at first—frightened of every man who came near her—but Dr. Hunter spoke to her so gently that she soon forgot her fears. He told her it might take several operations, but when he was finished, she would be beautiful again. And she was.'' A tear trickled down Rosa's cheek, and she quickly brushed it away.

Grace was more affected by the story than she wanted to admit. It was hard enough to do what had to be done, but when she thought of Rosa's daughter and of all the children Ethan had helped, Grace couldn't help asking herself if ridding the world of a man like Trevor Reardon was an equal exchange for depriving it of a doctor as talented as Ethan.

Not daring to ponder the question, Grace rose. "I'd better be going. I still have a million things to do."

Rosa nodded sympathetically and stood, too. Just as she started for the kitchen door to show Grace out, the phone rang.

Grace held up her hand. "Go ahead and get that. I can let myself out."

In the living room, she couldn't resist stopping by the parrot's cage. The two of them had formed some kind of strange bond, Grace decided. A sort of mutual disrespect for one another. Besides which, she needed something to take her mind off Rosa's story and the doubts it had created for her.

"So your name is Simon, huh? As in Simon Says?"

The bird cocked his head and stared at her.

Grace cocked her head and stared back. "Well, why don't you say it, Simon? I know you're dying to."

Simon blinked, but remained silent.

After a moment, Grace crooned, "They're not real, they're not real, they're not real. Come on, what do you say, Simon?"

The bird fluffed his wings importantly and squawked, "I say we get rid of the bastard once and for all."

SINCE AMY COLE had no family, Grace, in keeping with her cover, had taken care of all the funeral arrangements. She'd kept the service simple, ordering an elegant spray of white roses to rest atop the mahogany casket while a framed picture of Amy, the one from her apartment, was displayed on a nearby pedestal.

The small chapel was surprisingly crowded. Grace glanced around the room, trying to sort out who was who. Several people clustered around the apartment manager from Amy's complex, and Grace decided that most of them were probably Amy's neighbors. Some of the others were undoubtedly from work. But aside from the manager, Grace didn't recognize any of the mourners.

She glanced at her watch, wondering what was keeping Ethan. He'd been incommunicado with her all day, and although he'd been under surveillance for most of that time, Grace had yet to be given a report on his movements.

When ten more minutes had gone by and he still hadn't shown, she began to worry. Could something have happened? Had Reardon somehow managed to slip through the trap they'd set for him?

A sour taste rose in Grace's mouth at the thought. She wanted Reardon, but at what price? Two days ago, she would have said any price, but that was before she'd met Ethan. Before she'd allowed him to get to her.

Now she wasn't sure what she would do if the choice came down to Reardon or Ethan.

You're a fool, a little voice whispered inside her. *You don't know this man. You don't owe him anything.*

True, but in the last two days, he'd awakened something inside Grace she had thought forever dead. Feelings. Attraction.

Need.

She closed her eyes briefly as a wave of doubt rolled over her. She didn't want to need anyone. She couldn't afford to. Need was synonymous with vulnerability. Weakness. And Grace had to remain strong. She had to remain focused. If she didn't, she might not be able to save herself or Ethan.

But what if Reardon does manage to penetrate the screen? that same voice taunted her.

Grace told herself it was impossible. The plan would work.

But would it? Hadn't this operation already been full of surprises? Amy Cole was never supposed to die. In fact, she shouldn't have been anywhere near the clinic that night. Her cooperation with the FBI had been critical in formulating the plan to capture Trevor Reardon, but because Grace hadn't been honest, Amy had gotten scared. If Myra's hunch was right, Amy had gone to the clinic to warn Ethan that the Feds were on to him. And she'd gotten herself killed in the process.

Grace blamed herself for that. Though she wasn't a mind reader, she should have interpreted the signs. Amy was crazy in love with Ethan. When she suddenly realized what her cooperation with the authorities would mean for him—and for herself—she'd panicked. Grace should have seen it coming, but she'd never been the best judge of what love could do to you. What it could *make* you do.

In fact, she had been the very worst judge.

Not wanting to start an avalanche of memories, she turned her attention back to the crowd. A man had come in and gone straight to Amy's picture. He stood staring at it for a long moment, then walked over to the casket, running his fingers along the smooth surface of the lid. He began to sob quietly.

Uneasy, Grace watched him. Who was he? How had he known Amy? She'd told Grace she had no family or close friends, other than Ethan, but this man had obviously been deeply affected by her death.

Someone touched Grace's arm and she whirled. The chaplain, Bible clutched to his chest, stood at her side. He looked to be in his mid-forties, tall and thin with arrow-straight posture. His cheekbones were classically high, giving what would have been an otherwise plain face an almost regal look. His lips were thin, his nose a bit broad and his dark brown hair was streaked with gray. Grace thought he had the kindest eyes she'd ever seen, but even as that notion flitted through her mind, trepidation swept over her. Had she met him before?

He held out his hand to her, and Grace reluctantly took it. His handshake was warm and firm, not in the least offensive, but a shiver racked her just the same.

As soon as she deemed it appropriate, she withdrew her hand from his.

The chaplain smiled. "You're Amy's sister, I understand."

Grace hesitated. Lying in the service of her country was one thing, but deliberately deceiving a man of God something else. "We weren't close," she said carefully.

"That often happens in families. A rift occurs, time passes, and before anyone can imagine, it's too late. But take comfort in the knowledge that it never is really too late. You will see your sister again."

Grace's gaze fastened on the man's clerical collar. She realized suddenly why he seemed so familiar to her, why he made her so uneasy. She had not been around a clergyman since her family's funeral, but now she had a vivid recall of that day, of the minister from their church holding her hand, offering her comfort in the knowledge that she and her family would someday be reunited in the hereafter.

It was only later that Grace had decided her only comfort would come here on earth, when she put Trevor Reardon away forever.

The man at the coffin was still crying. The chaplain smiled sadly. "If you'll excuse me..."

Grace watched him approach the casket and put a gentle hand on the man's shoulder. The chaplain spoke to the weeping man softly, and after a bit, his sobs subsided. He turned and walked away from the casket, his gaze brushing Grace's before he seated himself at the back of the chapel.

It was nearing on four o'clock. Rosa came in and nodded to Grace before finding a seat near the front. The group of people from Amy's apartment complex settled near the middle. Others scattered about the remaining pews. Just as the chaplain took the podium, two last-minute arrivals started everyone whispering among themselves.

Grace recognized the woman at once. Pilar Hunter had looked exquisitely beautiful in the pictures Grace had seen of her, but in person, the woman was breathtaking.

Unlike almost everyone else in the chapel, she'd refused to wear black, choosing instead a sleeveless dress in dusky blue linen that did incredible things to her dark hair and eyes. The hemline was short, her heels high, and her bare legs went on forever. Grace couldn't help glancing down at her own attire—a simple silk jersey dress that she had once thought flattering. For the first time that afternoon, she was almost glad Ethan hadn't shown up.

The man with Pilar took her elbow and guided her toward a pew. They settled directly behind Grace, and she caught a strong whiff of Pilar's perfume—a heavy, exotic scent that seemed to capture the essence of the woman herself.

As the chaplain started the service, Grace became increasingly aware of Pilar's presence, as if the woman was staring at the back of Grace's head. She remembered what Ethan had said about his wife, that she seemed like a woman capable of throwing acid on his car or in his face. Grace understood what he meant. In the brief glimpse she'd had of Pilar, Grace had sensed an undercurrent of suppressed violence that was almost as tangible as her perfume.

I say we just kill the bastard and be done with it.

Could she and Myra have been wrong? Grace wondered suddenly. What if Trevor Reardon hadn't been behind the attack in Ethan's clinic? What if someone else wanted him dead?

Grace tried to put the notion out of her head. She couldn't afford to get sidetracked or to let down her guard. That was exactly what Reardon would want. For all she knew, he might be in this very room now, watching her from a distance and laughing. Laughing…

Grace looked up and her gaze met the chaplain's. He smiled at her and nodded almost imperceptibly before he bowed his head to pray for Amy Cole's immortal soul.

Chapter Eight

Ethan stared at the pile of shoes on his bedroom floor as a headache beat a painful staccato inside his brain.

What the hell was going on here?

Why didn't any of these shoes fit him?

His movements almost frantic, Ethan tried on another pair, and then another. Every shoe in his closet was too small for him. The only pair that fit him were the ones he'd been wearing the night he woke up in the hospital, the ones he'd been wearing ever since.

The loafers had been fine with casual clothes, but today, getting dressed for Amy's funeral, he'd found a black suit, white shirt, and somber tie in the closet. When he'd brought out the appropriate shoes, he'd discovered they were too small for him, as was every other pair of shoes in the closet.

He didn't understand why. Granted, the clothes he'd been wearing were loose, but that could be explained by weight loss following surgery. And he knew he'd had the appendectomy because he had the scar to prove it. The dreams of being shot, of falling off a cliff were just that—drug induced visions. The memory loss was due to the blow to his head. His wariness of the authorities—well, Grace had explained that to him as well.

Clearly, everything that had happened to him had a logical, if disturbing, explanation.

Except for the fact that none of his shoes fit.

Ethan picked up the black dress shoe and studied it. Why would he—why would *anyone*—buy dozens of pairs of expensive shoes in the wrong size? It made no sense—

Without warning, the pain in his head became razor-sharp, blinding. Dropping the shoe, Ethan put his hands to his head, pressing tightly as he squeezed his eyes closed.

An image shot through him. He could see someone running for his life through a jungle. He could smell the dank scent of the vegetation, feel the cloying heat, hear the sounds of pursuit behind him. He *knew* the man's fear. But the man's face was not the one Ethan stared at in the mirror.

And yet...

The man in the vision was him and it wasn't.

Unlike the picture that Ethan had seen of himself downstairs in the study, he felt connected to the man running through the jungle. He knew him in a way he did not know the stranger staring back at him from the mirror.

But...why?

Why was he having another man's visions?

Why did none of the shoes in his closet fit him?

Why was he in possession of a gun that may well have been issued to someone in one of the special forces of the military? Someone like an elite Navy SEAL? Someone like Trevor Reardon?

Why did a plastic surgeon know how to use a weapon like that?

An explanation came with another blinding flash of light.

Pain exploded inside Ethan's head, and for a moment, he thought he was going to be sick.

WHEN THE SERVICE was over, Grace looked up to find Ethan standing in the doorway of the chapel. As his gaze met hers, she felt a physical jolt. It was almost as if a bolt of pure adrenaline had ping-ponged between them.

He looked pale, Grace thought with sudden anxiety. Shaken. What had happened to him?

She got up and started toward him, but was waylaid several times by well-wishers—first by the apartment manager, then by a neighbor, and then by Rosa, whose initial frost toward Grace had thawed. The housekeeper squeezed Grace's hand comfortingly, then, her glance moving over Grace's shoulder, she pursed her lips in stern disapproval.

Grace followed her gaze to find Pilar and her escort on a collision course with Ethan. Wondering if an unpleasant scene was about to erupt, Grace glanced around the room. Most of the mourners had filed out of the chapel by this time. The grieving man remained seated, his head bowed in silent prayer, while the chaplain stood at his podium, waiting for everyone to leave. The late afternoon sun shining through the stained glass window behind the clergyman gave him an almost angelic appearance. The image should have been comforting, but for some reason it was not.

Hoping to abort a possible spectacle, Grace walked

over to stand beside Ethan. Their gazes met again, but neither of them said anything.

Pilar stared at her coolly. Even this close, Grace couldn't find a single imperfection in the woman's complexion.

"So you're Amy Cole's sister." Her voice, light and musical, was as attractive as the rest of her, and the Spanish accent gave her a hint of mystery. "I'm Pilar. Ethan's wife." The slight emphasis on the last word made Grace wonder again about Ethan and Pilar's relationship.

"How do you do?" Grace extended her hand, but the woman's fingertips barely brushed against her palm.

Pilar stared at her critically. "You don't look anything like her, you know."

Grace assumed the comment was meant to cut. "My sister was very beautiful," she said.

Pilar raised her narrow shoulders in an elegant shrug. "In a trampish sort of way."

For the first time, Ethan stirred to life beside Grace. "For God's sake, she's dead. Can't you show a little respect?"

Pilar's dark brows rose in mild outrage. "The same respect she showed for our marriage vows?"

"Why did you come here?" Ethan demanded. He turned to the man standing next to Pilar. "Why did you let her come?"

The man laughed softly. "You don't 'let' Pilar do anything. You should know that better than anyone." He turned to Grace and put out his hand. "By the way, I'm Bob Kendall. I'm very sorry about your sister."

So this was Ethan's ex-partner. Unlike Pilar's, his

handshake was firm, and his fingers lingered against Grace's for just a moment too long.

She instantly disliked him. He was too smooth, and his gray eyes were too insincere.

He said to Ethan, "Are you feeling all right, buddy? You look a little pale."

"I'm fine," Ethan said tersely.

"Still, it might not hurt to give Mancetti a call. I don't imagine she was too happy to learn you'd checked yourself out of the hospital."

Ethan didn't answer. Instead he turned to Grace, muttering, "When can we get out of here?"

She shrugged, feeling Pilar's dark eyes scouring her. "Now. I've made arrangements for a private burial."

Ethan nodded. His eyes were shadowed. Haunted. Was it Amy's funeral that had gotten to him? Had he finally remembered her? Remembered that…he cared for her?

Ethan turned toward the door, but Pilar caught his arm. "You can't just walk off like this. We're not through, Ethan."

He stared down at her for a long moment, then very deliberately removed her hand from his arm. "You could have fooled me."

OUTSIDE, THE SUNLIGHT, even at five o'clock, was still brutal. Ethan pulled a pair of dark glasses from the inside of his suit coat and slipped them on. He hadn't been able to rid himself of the headache. A handful of aspirin had dulled the pain, but the confusion whirling inside him was still as strong as ever.

Beside him, Grace tried to match her steps to his, but he had a good eight inches on her. He slowed, then stopped altogether in the shade of a huge water oak.

The lower limbs were so heavy, they'd been braced to keep from snapping. Spanish moss dripped silvery green from the gnarled branches, giving the tree a forlorn, almost ghostly appearance. In the distance, the cars in the parking lot wavered in the rising heat from the pavement. Their inconsistency seemed surreal and out of place, but the eeriness matched Ethan's mood.

Grace said a little breathlessly, "What happened to you? I was beginning to worry."

He gazed down at her. "Were you?"

"Of course. You know as well as I do the danger you're in."

"Do I?"

A brief frown flitted across her features. "What happened, Ethan? Why were you so late getting to the service?"

The way she said his name, in a voice that was just the tiniest bit husky, made him want more than ever to discount his earlier thoughts. But the question was like a mantra inside his head.

Who am I? Who the hell am I?

He studied Grace's features, thinking how lovely she looked today, and how very calm she seemed for having just come from her sister's funeral. Her mood was somber, as was the black dress she wore, but there was something about her eyes—an alertness, an intensity—that mystified him and made him believe he wasn't the only one who had secrets.

He took her arm and drew her deeper into the shadow of the oak tree. "What if I told you, I'm not the man you think I am?"

Her eyes instantly deepened. "What do you mean?"

He paused, wondering what to say, how to tell her

his suspicions. *I may not be Dr. Ethan Hunter. In fact, I may be...*

He couldn't even finish the thought. His heart began to beat wildly against his chest. Ethan was sure he'd never felt so alone, so out of control, so lost as he did at that moment.

And Grace. God help him, he was still drawn to her. Still attracted to her. Still *wanted* her. In some perverse way, more than ever because he knew if what he feared was true, he could never have her.

In fact, it might even come down to the basic choice of his life...or hers.

She was still staring up at him, her incredible blue eyes deep and intense. He wondered what she was thinking, if she had even an inkling of what he was feeling.

She touched his arm. The action made Ethan almost groan out loud.

"Have you remembered something?"

"No. But what if I told you—" He wanted to tell her about the shoes, and possibly the gun, but a movement at the entrance of the chapel drew his attention. A man came out of the building and paused, looking around. Ethan dimly recognized him from the funeral service. He'd been seated at the back, weeping quietly, when Ethan had arrived.

Ethan glanced at him, then turned his gaze back to Grace. But out of the corner of his eye, he saw the man start toward them.

"Do you know who that man is?" he asked Grace suddenly.

She turned, following his gaze, and Ethan saw her tense. "No. I saw him inside, though. He was pretty torn up."

Ethan watched as the man approached them. He had the kind of face that made it hard to judge his age, but something about the way he walked, the way he dressed—casually in khaki pants and a button-down collar shirt—gave Ethan the impression that he was fairly young, no more than late thirties. The receding hairline was probably premature, as were the lines around his eyes and mouth.

As he neared them, Ethan heard Grace catch her breath. He thought that her gasp was not because she suddenly recognized the man, but because of the look of unadulterated fury on his face. Ethan saw Grace's hand slip inside her purse, but before he could wonder about her intentions, the man stepped up to him. He was shorter than Ethan by only an inch or so, but their builds were similar. They stood almost chest to chest.

"Dr. Ethan Hunter?"

"Yes?"

Without warning, the man hauled off and punched Ethan square in the face. Pain flashed white-hot over his already bruised flesh, and as Ethan staggered back a step, red-hot anger shot through him. Almost instinctively, he lunged at the man, but Grace jumped between them.

"Stop it!" she ordered, putting a hand on each of their chests with surprising strength and authority. She turned to the stranger. "Why did you do that?" she demanded.

The man's gaze was still furious. "He had it coming!"

Ethan said coldly, "The hell I did. I don't even know who you are."

The man glared at him. "Of course, you wouldn't remember me. Why should you? I was nobody important, just the man Amy was going to marry, that's all. Until you came along."

Grace must have sensed the anger welling inside him again, for she gave him a shove. "Calm down," she said. "This is not the place for violence."

The man looked immediately contrite. His blue eyes flooded with tears. "No, you're right. Amy wouldn't have wanted that."

He took a few steps away from Grace and Ethan, as if struggling to gather his composure. But he continued to glare at Ethan. "We did meet once. I guess you don't remember. I came to Amy's apartment to beg her to come back to me, but...it was too late. You'd already seduced her away from me."

The raw pain in the man's eyes made Ethan's stomach knot. He didn't know whether he was really Dr. Ethan Hunter or not, but at that moment, the one thing he was certain of was that he didn't much care for Dr. Hunter or the way he treated people.

Grace said softly, "I didn't know Amy was ever engaged. She never mentioned it."

"That's odd," the man said, wiping at his eyes. "Because she never mentioned having a sister, either."

GRACE COULD FEEL Ethan's gaze on her, but she kept her eyes trained on the man before her. Something about him seemed very pitiful to her. He was not unattractive, but the way he dressed, the receding hairline, the ordinary features must have made him feel like a moth to Amy's butterfly. No wonder he harbored such animosity toward Ethan. He was the epitome of everything this man was not.

Grace said carefully, "Amy and I were estranged for

several years. We hadn't spoken with each other until very recently.''

''I guess that explains why she never wanted to talk about her family.'' The man stuck out his hand. ''My name's Danny Medford.''

''Grace Donovan. You already know Dr. Hunter,'' she said with irony.

He shot Ethan a killing glance before turning back to Grace. ''I don't suppose it would be possible—'' He broke off, looking ill at ease.

''What?'' Grace prompted.

Danny looked at her hopefully. ''Do you think we could get together sometime? You know, to talk about Amy?''

He seemed a nice enough guy, but Grace had no wish to perpetuate the deception, to contribute in any way to the man's pain. However, with Ethan looking on, she had little choice but to keep up the farce. ''I'd like that. Maybe in a few weeks when it isn't so painful to talk about her.''

He nodded, smiling wistfully as he fished a card from his shirt pocket and handed it to her. ''That's my work number. I'm there at all hours. Feel free to call anytime.''

Medford Engineering, the card read. Grace slipped it in her purse and smiled. ''It's been nice meeting you, Danny.''

''Likewise.'' He turned to Ethan. ''I wouldn't be surprised if you and I meet again someday.''

There was no mistaking the threat in the man's words, but Ethan merely shrugged. ''I'll be ready next time.''

After the man had disappeared into the parking lot,

Ethan fished a handkerchief from his pocket and wiped away the trickle of blood at the corner of his mouth.

"Yet another of Dr. Hunter's enemies," he said enigmatically, watching the man's battered Toyota sedan pull out of the parking lot. "They seem to be coming out of the woodwork."

"He seems harmless enough."

Ethan lifted a brow as he daubed at his lip. "Easy for you to say."

Grace almost smiled. "I meant comparatively speaking. The enemy we really have to worry about is Trevor Reardon."

"I wonder." Ethan's eyes grew dark and distant, as if he'd gone someplace in his mind that Grace had no wish to follow. Or had he gone to a place she'd already been to?

There was still blood on his lip. She took the handkerchief from his hand. "Here, let me."

She blotted the droplet of blood as gently as she could, but Ethan winced at her touch. He took her hand and pulled it away. For a moment they stood that way, her hand in his, eyes locked, until Grace's stomach began to flutter wildly.

She was accustomed to butterflies. She got them the first day of every new assignment, every time she had to draw her weapon, or when she faced danger. But this was different, because the greater threat was coming, not from Ethan, but from within herself.

She shivered, watching him. So much about him she didn't know, but the one thing that was all too real was her attraction to him. Her feelings for him. She couldn't explain them. They made no sense. But the emotions raging inside her were so real and so intense, that if he were to kiss her at that moment, Grace knew she would have no willpower to resist.

What few relationships she'd had over the years had been with men who had no expectations of a future with her. There could be no future with Ethan, either, and yet Grace found herself yearning for something she'd never wanted before. The hollowness inside her heart made her feel lost and lonely in a way she hadn't felt in a long, long time.

She almost hated Ethan for that. Hated him for making her lose confidence in her ability to do what needed to be done. For making her want him.

Grace closed her eyes, letting the heat of the day wash over her. The humidity curled the fine hairs at the back of her neck, and she could feel the silk of her dress clinging to her body. She had a sudden image of cool water lapping at her toes. Of a fragrant breeze rippling through her hair. Of a man lying naked beside her, whispering in her ear…

When she opened her eyes, Ethan was staring down at her so intently, Grace thought he must have read her mind. She caught her breath.

"What are we going to do about this, Grace?"

She didn't try to misconstrue his meaning. The sparks between them were all too obvious. "There's nothing to be done. We just have to…ignore it, I guess."

"You think that's possible?" His eyes darkened, so much so that Grace had to glance away. She had to find a way to subdue the power he had over her.

"It has to be, because as you pointed out yesterday, you're a married man. Just because you can't remember your wife doesn't mean you don't still have feelings for her. You might even still love her."

He almost laughed. "Do you really believe that?"

Grace remembered the coldness in Pilar's expression, the emptiness in her eyes, and she shuddered. "I don't think you still love her. Maybe you never did, but it doesn't change the fact that you are still married to her. I don't take that lightly, Ethan."

"I wish I could say the same." Grace didn't think he was trying to be facetious. His eyes were too haunted for that.

"And that brings us back to Amy," she said quietly. "I don't want to be another one of your conquests. I won't be."

"I don't even remember Amy," he said. "Everything you've told me about her…it doesn't even seem real. It's like…someone else had the affair with her. Someone else married Pilar. It wasn't me. I'm not that man."

Grace wished she knew what to say to him, but she didn't. She wished suddenly that what he was telling her was true—that he wasn't Dr. Ethan Hunter, but someone entirely different. Someone free and honorable. Someone with whom she just might have a second shot at life.

But reality and fantasy were two different concepts, and no one knew that better than Grace.

"Ethan—"

"I'm *not* that man, Grace."

He could almost convince her when he looked at her that way. When he skimmed his knuckles along the side of her cheek, brushed back the hair from her face with a touch so gentle, Grace could have wept. She closed her eyes briefly, wanting him to kiss her with every fiber of her being, and knowing all the while that if he did, there would be no chance for her then. Everything in her world would be lost.

She took a step back from him. "Losing memories doesn't change who you are. What you've done."

"What I've done." The shadow in his eyes deepened. He raked his fingers through his hair, turning away from her. "There's nothing that will ever change that."

"No, but there is such a thing as redemption. Restitution."

His gaze came back to meet hers. "And how do you propose I pay for my sins?" he asked grimly.

Grace shrugged. "Helping me bring a man like Trevor Reardon to justice is a good place to start."

Ethan's expression hardened. Something that Grace couldn't quite define flashed in his eyes. "That sounds so naive, but somehow you don't strike me as the Pollyanna type. I may not remember who I am or what I've done, but I don't think I'm the only one here with secrets."

Grace's heartbeat quickened. "What do you mean?"

He gazed down at her, studying her. "I don't know who you are any more than I know who I am. We're strangers, and yet…we seem to have some kind of…connection. Even you can't deny that."

"Maybe our connection is Amy," Grace tried to say calmly.

He shook his head. "I don't think so. I can't help but wonder if you're holding something back from me."

"Like what?"

He hesitated. His gaze grew even more pensive. "Did we know each other before?"

"No." Grace's heart pounded like a piston. He was

getting too close. His suspicions were mounting by the minute, and she didn't know what to do to stop them. If he found out who she was...how she was using him...

God help you if you're lying to me.

"I told you before," she said. "We'd never met until that night outside the hospital."

"Then what is this connection we have?" he asked almost urgently.

Grace shrugged. "Attraction. Chemistry. Call it what you like, but that's all it is."

"Why do I feel as if it's something more?" Ethan grabbed her forearms and pulled her toward him. "Why do I feel as if I know you better than I could ever know the woman who claims to be my wife? Why do I know how your lips would taste if I kissed you right now? How your body would feel beneath mine if we—"

"Please don't," Grace said breathlessly. She put her hands to his chest, but it was a meaningless gesture. She wasn't going to push him away. It took every ounce of her strength not to pull him closer.

"You feel it, too. I can see it your eyes."

"Please—"

He drew her so close, their lips were only a heartbeat apart. "You want me to kiss you," he said almost accusingly. "Almost as much as I want to."

"Ethan—"

The space between them evaporated. "Tell me to stop," he murmured against her mouth.

Grace said nothing. Instead she closed her eyes and waited for the inevitable to happen. Waited for her life to come tumbling down around her. When it didn't, her relief—or was it disappointment?—was so intense, her head spun dizzily. She opened her eyes and gazed up at him.

Something glimmered in his eyes, something that looked almost like triumph. He dropped his hands from her shoulders and backed away. "I told you it wouldn't be easy," he said, in a tone that sounded more like a threat than a warning.

GRACE LAY IN bed that night, wide awake and listening to the street noises outside her hotel. The room was dimly illuminated by streetlights and neon signs that caused shadows to leap and cavort across the walls and ceiling, like demons celebrating some dark victory.

Earlier, she'd opened the curtains so that she could see the balcony outside the sliding glass doors. Airplane lights twinkled in the night sky, and between the slats of the balcony railing, she could see the faint movement of pine boughs stirring in the breeze. She would have liked to open the doors, letting in the breeze and the scent of evergreen, but she never slept with the windows open. Her doors and windows were always closed and always locked.

Grace stared out into the darkness and thought about Ethan, wondering what he was doing tonight. His house was under surveillance and secured by a state-of-the-art alarm system that even an FBI agent couldn't find fault with. There was no reason for Grace to worry, and yet she *was* worried. She couldn't shake the uneasiness that had invaded her thoughts since she'd left Ethan at the chapel this afternoon.

I'm not that man, Grace.

What had he meant by that? What had he meant when he'd said, *What if I told you I'm not the man you think I am?*

Was it wishful thinking on his part? The denial of a man with no memory learning things about himself that were more than just unpleasant?

No wonder he was so confused. The man who altered criminals' faces for money was a direct contradiction to the man Rosa had told Grace about earlier. A man who could transform hideous monsters into angels. A man who changed children's lives forever.

Was Ethan Hunter a saint with a badly tarnished halo, or a Dr. Jekyll and Mr. Hyde—a man with two entirely different sides to his personality?

Grace shivered in the gloom, considering all the possibilities but trying not to dwell on the one thing Ethan had said that perhaps troubled her the most.

Why do I feel as if I know you better than I could ever know the woman who claims to be my wife? Why do I know how your lips would taste if I kissed you right now? How your body would feel beneath mine if we—

Grace sucked in a long breath, trying to remember her objectives, but the situation had taken a turn she couldn't have anticipated. It had seemed so easy when she and Myra had first devised the plan. Come to Houston. Set up surveillance and a cover for Grace. Wait for Dr. Ethan Hunter to arrive from Mexico and then approach him. Convince him to cooperate so that Trevor Reardon could be drawn out into the open.

But then everything had gone wrong. It had all happened too quickly. Ethan had come back from Mexico weeks earlier than planned, before complete backup and support were in place. And then Amy Cole had died. The entire operation had had to be hastily revised, and now everything hinged on Grace's ability to perpetuate her deception. To remain close to Ethan.

But what happened when it was all over? Originally, Grace hadn't stopped to consider what would happen to Ethan once Reardon was safely behind bars again. Or dead.

But Ethan had his own sins to answer for, and leniency would depend on the extent of his cooperation. Grace hadn't thought to be involved in anything beyond Reardon's capture, but now she realized how difficult it would be to walk away, to never look back, to betray a man she was deeply attracted to.

For a moment, she considered calling Myra and asking for advice, but somehow Grace thought this was beyond the older agent's field of expertise. She didn't think Myra had ever been torn like this. Grace couldn't even imagine Myra Temple falling in love.

She couldn't imagine herself falling in love, either. Though it was true she was attracted to Ethan, that they shared a connection she couldn't begin to explain, it certainly wasn't love. It couldn't be love because Grace was immune to that emotion. She'd promised herself a long time ago that she would never again be vulnerable, and love made you vulnerable. It made you weak. It made you forget who you were and what you had to do.

Grace knew exactly who she was. She was a federal agent on the trail of a ruthless killer. And she knew what she was. A woman who would do anything to bring down the man who had nearly destroyed her.

Ethan Hunter could not be allowed to get in her way. She would use him and she would betray him. And in the end, she would walk away from him.

SOMETIME AFTER TWO in the morning, Grace managed to doze off. But her dreams were filled with distorted images from her past and her present. She saw Trevor Reardon smiling down at her, but before she had time to draw her weapon, his face turned into Ethan's. And he was still smiling. Still taunting her.

Grace hovered in that nether realm of dream and reality. She knew she was still sleeping, but she was powerless to control the images playing themselves out in her mind.

In her dream, the phone was ringing. As if watching a movie, she saw herself pick up the receiver and lift it to her ear. "Hello?"

There was no response, but she could tell someone was on the other end. She caught her breath, waiting, while a fine sense of dread seeped over her. "Who's there?"

Silence.

Then a deep, seductive voice said in her ear, "I liked what you were wearing at the funeral today, Grace. Black becomes you."

They were almost the exact words Trevor Reardon had spoken to her fourteen years ago, after her family's funeral. Fear exploded inside Grace, and she gasped in horror.

Wake up! It's only a dream! she tried to warn herself.

Some part of her knew that it was a nightmare, but Grace was powerless to break free of it. She tried to fight her way to consciousness, but it was as if invisible hands were holding her down, pulling her more deeply into sleep.

It all seemed so frighteningly real. Grace heard herself say, "Where are you?"

And that sensuous voice replying, "Closer than you think."

"How close?"

Another pause, then, "You still favor pearls, I see."

There was something about his voice, something that triggered a flash of insight. Grace struggled through the layers of sleep, trying to cling to that elusive revelation that had come to her in the dream.

Something about his voice…

Yes! That was it! She'd heard that same voice recently, only…somehow it had been different, distorted. She hadn't recognized it because he'd disguised it.

As the cobwebs of sleep began to clear, Grace lay beneath the covers, trembling. The dream lingered. The fear it generated made her head swim, and she couldn't think straight. For a moment, Grace considered fixing herself a drink to steady her nerves, but that wouldn't help. It never had before.

She glanced at the nightstand beside the bed, wondering what time it was. In the glow of the clock face, she saw the tiny pearl studs she'd worn to Amy's funeral yesterday.

Forcing herself to get up, Grace crossed the room to the window and stared out into the gloom. Dawn was breaking over the city, and she could see a fleet of low-lying clouds moving in from the coast. The castoff glow of the sun, still hidden below the horizon, tinted the edges with a golden pink that gradually deepened to violet.

It was that strange time of morning, before the sun came up, when the shadows outside deepened and the night terrors had yet to flee.

Grace's first instinct was to run. To pack her bags and leave the city as fast as she could. And that impulse surprised her. She'd thought about this operation long and hard, even before she'd learned Reardon had escaped from prison a second time. She used to daydream about meeting him face to face. She used to picture his features on the targets she destroyed with her pistol at Quantico and wonder what it would be like to look him in the eye the exact moment she put a bullet through his heart.

Reardon's face would be different now, but somehow Grace had thought she would know him anywhere. She'd wanted to believe that the evil inside his soul would radiate from his body like an oily, black aura, but no one she'd met recently had aroused that kind of suspicion in her. She'd even considered the possibility that Reardon was hundreds, perhaps thousands of miles away, and that whoever had killed Amy and had tried to kill Ethan was someone else. Pilar or Kendall or even, as the police thought, a stranger looking for drugs.

But Grace had no more doubts. She was sure now that she'd heard Reardon's voice recently, but she couldn't think where. At Amy's funeral? She'd talked to a lot of people there she hadn't known, men and women who claimed to be friends and acquaintances of Amy's. Had one of them been Trevor Reardon? Had she been that close to him? Had he...touched her?

Grace shuddered in revulsion. Obviously, Reardon had managed to disguise his voice well enough to fool her for a while, but there was a quality about it that couldn't be altered. In her sleep, Grace had remembered that quality.

Was he out there somewhere? Was he watching her even now? Was he finding her in the crosshairs of a high-powered weapon, laughing all the while at her foolishness? Her weakness?

Grace's insides quivered with fear and dread, but she

forced herself to remain at the window. She was safe for the time being. Reardon wouldn't shoot her here. Not from a distance. He enjoyed killing too much. For him, death was a personal experience. An intimate one. He would want to enjoy it to its fullest potential.

When he came for her this time, Grace knew it would be more for pleasure than revenge.

Chapter Nine

"Buenos días," Rosa greeted the next morning. She stood back so Grace could enter.

"Good morning, Rosa. Is Ethan in?"

"He's upstairs in his study."

She led Grace up the stairway and through the living room, then tapping on the study door, she opened it a crack and announced Grace's arrival.

Ethan was sitting behind his desk, studying a legal document that was several pages thick. When Grace entered the room, he looked up. "Morning. Or is it still morning?"

"Barely." Grace glanced at her watch. "It's just after eleven."

Ethan's eyes looked a bit unfocused, and his lower face was shadowed with beard. Grace wondered if he'd been to bed at all last night, or if like her, his sleep had been plagued with nightmares. Self-doubts.

He glanced at Rosa still hovering in the doorway. "You can leave whenever you need to. Don't worry about me. I'll manage just fine."

Rosa's dark eyes darted from Ethan to Grace, but this morning she didn't appear to be as disapproving. Grace wondered if she'd managed to win the housekeeper over, but if she had, it was a hollow victory because it had been won by deception.

Rosa shrugged. "*Adiós* then. I'll see you in a few days."

After she'd gone, Grace turned back to Ethan. "Where's she going?"

"Her grandson is sick, and her daughter needs help so I gave her some time off. Under the circumstances, I thought it a good idea to get her out of the house for a few days." His ominous words reminded Grace all too clearly of the dream she'd had last night.

"As a matter of fact," Ethan said, "I've been thinking about your safety as well. I want to talk to you about something."

He seemed different this morning, and Grace's first thought was that he'd gotten his memory back. "What about?"

"I realized this morning that I've never even been to your apartment. I don't even know where you live."

Grace frowned. "So?"

"So...how safe is it? Do you have a security system? A gated entry? A guard who patrols the grounds?" Ethan sat forward suddenly, his dark eyes intense. "If Reardon is watching my every move as you seem to think, then he knows you and I are working together. He knows you're Amy's sister. He may even know where you live."

There was no doubt in Grace's mind that Trevor Reardon knew where she was. Not after last night. "We can't do anything about that," she said, evading Ethan's questions. "But believe me, I take every precaution. You don't have to worry about me."

"But I do worry." His eyes deepened, and Grace could have sworn his gaze dropped to her mouth. She couldn't help remembering the way his lips had felt against hers. "What precautions do you take? Do you own a gun?"

She forced herself to hold his gaze. If she looked away, she would be admitting her discomfort. "Why do you ask?"

He shrugged. "It's a logical question. How are you going to catch Reardon if you don't have a weapon?"

Grace hesitated. "All right, yes, I have a gun. And before you ask, yes, I do know how to use it."

"Why does that not surprise me?" he muttered.

"I've also taken some self-defense courses." She wasn't sure why she added that except perhaps to let him know that if push came to shove, she could more than hold her own—against Reardon or anyone else.

"Somehow I think it may take more than a karate chop to bring down an assassin turned terrorist," he said dryly.

Grace almost allowed herself a smile. "That's what the gun is for."

Their gazes met. Something that might have been admiration glimmered in his eyes. "Still, I think you'd be safer, maybe we'd both be safer, if you moved in here with me. The security system is first rate, and besides—what was it you said the other day? You watch my back and I'll watch yours? It would be easier to do that if we were both in the same location."

She wasn't sure why his words surprised her so much. Maybe because when she'd hinted the same thing that first night, he'd made it all too clear that he had no intention of inviting her to stay in his home. Now, he was acting as if the idea was his and that it made all the sense in the world.

Grace knew she should leap at the chance to move

in with him. Her main function in this whole operation was to get as close—and stay as close—as she could to Ethan so that when Reardon came after him, she would be ready. But now she had to wonder if proximity to Ethan would be such a good idea. Would she be able to remain alert and focused, or would her attraction to him make her careless? Reckless?

A shiver of awareness slipped over her.

"What's wrong?" he asked. "You know as well as I do it makes sense for us to stick together."

"Yes, I know, but—"

"But what?" His gaze became even more penetrating. "Are you afraid to move in here? Are you afraid of me?"

"No. Of course not," she said almost too quickly. "I'm not afraid of you."

"Then who are you afraid of? Reardon? Yourself, maybe?"

Grace felt a prickle of anger at his assumption. "Contrary to what you seem to think, I'm not the least bit worried that I won't be able to constrain myself in your presence."

Amusement flashed in his eyes. "Then what's the problem?"

"A little thing called appearances," she said. "What will your neighbors think if I move in here with you? You're still married, Ethan."

"Not anymore." He picked up the blue-backed legal document from his desk and handed it to her.

"What is this?" she asked doubtfully.

"A courier delivered it this morning. It's a final divorce decree." Something very subtle changed in his voice. "As of today, I'm a free man, Grace."

She took the document and skimmed the front page.

"I don't know whether to offer my congratulations or my condolences," she tried to say lightly.

One dark brow arched. "You've met Pilar."

When Grace said nothing, he sat back in his chair and his eyes grew pensive. "It's strange to have proof of the ending of a marriage I don't even remember. But I guess this explains why Pilar was so eager to clean out the cash from the safe. A little something extra added to the settlement."

Grace handed the document back to him. "Have you heard from her?"

"No, and I don't expect to. Unless I see her tonight."

"Tonight?"

He paused. "A woman called me this morning. She said her name was Alina Torres. She talked for five minutes straight before I finally figured out she's Hun...my secretary."

"What did she want?" Grace asked.

"She reminded me that I have an invitation to some sort of charity benefit tonight at the Huntington Hotel. The proceeds will go directly into a building fund for a new children's wing at St. Mary's Hospital. According to Alina, I'd previously sent my regrets because I hadn't planned to be in town, but now that I'm back, she thought it would be a good idea for me to go. It seems I'm being presented with some sort of citation."

Grace's frown deepened. "Do you want to go?"

"Not particularly. But I've been thinking about what you said the other day. That the best way to draw out Reardon, or whoever wants to kill me, is to go about my normal business. The event tonight is written up in the paper today. If Reardon is keeping tabs on my activities, then he's bound to see it."

Ethan handed Grace a folded newspaper, and she read the headline.

Gala to Honor Dr. Ethan Hunter's Work with Underprivileged Children

He was right, she thought. A public event like this was just the sort of thing that would appeal to Reardon's macabre sense of humor. Still, she felt compelled to warn Ethan. "It could be dangerous. It would be very easy for Reardon to slip in with the crowd unnoticed. Especially since we don't even know what he looks like anymore."

"Isn't that the idea?" Ethan scowled. "I'm supposed to be a target, right?"

Yes. And the end justifies the means, Grace tried to tell herself. But even so, her first inclination was to try and talk him out of going. To somehow convince him to stay here, inside his fortress, where the locks and alarms just might keep him safe.

Out there, he *would* be a target. Bait for Reardon. And there was no guarantee Grace would be able to protect him. She wasn't even sure she could protect herself against Reardon.

She drew a long breath. "Is there any way you can get me an invitation?"

"I'm way ahead of you," he said. "Alina is sending over a ticket today, but you won't be seated on the dais with me."

"That's fine. It's better if I'm in the back, so I can keep an eye on the entire room."

He studied her for a moment, then his gaze dropped to the purse in her lap. "You'll be armed, I take it?"

She nodded. "Under the circumstances, I wouldn't leave home without it."

Their gazes held for what seemed an eternity, but in reality was hardly more than a second or two. But in the space of a heartbeat, Grace saw something in Ethan's eyes that she knew was mirrored in her own. Excitement. Anticipation. The thrill of the hunt.

They were suddenly two kindred spirits embarking on a perilous journey together. A journey that would be fraught with danger, intrigue and, because of the danger, passion.

Passion heightened by the knowledge that for them, tomorrow and regret might never come.

HE LIKED WHAT she was wearing. Her gown was midnight-blue, shot through with silver threads that shimmered in the light. She'd fastened a glittering clip in her hair that helped to glamorize the simple style, and her lips were tinted a dark, enticing red.

Ethan and Grace stood in the regal ballroom of the Huntington Hotel, their images reflected by the dozens of gilt-framed mirrors lining the walls. Overhead, twinkling chandeliers cast a rich ambience over the hall, while the tinkle of champagne glasses and the sound of muted laughter further enhanced the mood.

Ivory candles flickered on round tables covered with fine linen and set with gold-rimmed china, sparkling crystal and silverware polished to a gleaming finish.

Ethan, gazing at Grace, thought that she had been created for candlelight. The soft, dancing light brought out the drama of her features, deepening the blue of her eyes and igniting the red highlights in her hair.

She met his gaze briefly, then turned away, but not before he'd seen the desire in her eyes, in the tantalizing way she parted her deep red lips. Ever since she'd met him earlier at his house before coming here, the sparks had been flying between them.

Ethan's gaze slipped over her, moving from those lips to the pale skin of her throat, and then lower, to the lush curves outlined by the silky fabric of her gown.

Impulsively, he leaned toward her and whispered against her ear, "If you're carrying a concealed weapon in that dress, you're incredibly creative. And I mean that as a compliment."

He saw her smile, and realized, with something of a shock, that he'd never seen her do so before. She was always so serious, so…intense. Was she that way in every facet of her life?

Grace held up a glittering evening bag. "Don't worry. I told you I'd come prepared."

"And you were so right." His gaze moved over her again, and he wondered if he'd ever been as aware of a woman's allure as he was Grace's tonight.

Don't, a little voice warned him. *Don't get involved in something you can't finish. You don't even know who the hell you are.*

The tuxedo he'd pulled from the closet earlier fit him well enough, but like all the other clothing he'd worn, it wasn't a perfect fit. Nothing in Ethan Hunter's life was a perfect fit, except maybe for the way he felt about Grace.

He'd known from the first there was something special about her, something…intriguing about her, but her appeal was far more than just the physical attraction he felt for her. He'd meant what he said yesterday. They were connected to each other. He just didn't know how or why.

He touched her arm and felt her tense. "Would you like some champagne?"

Grace's gaze focused on the tray of sparkling wine as a waiter hovered nearby. "Maybe later. I want to keep a clear head tonight." All around them, people were starting to find their seats. Grace nodded toward the dais at the front of the room. "I think they're waiting for you."

"Wish me luck."

For a split second, he considered leaning down and kissing her, but then thought better of it. But when he would have turned away, she caught his arm at the last moment. Her blue eyes deepened on him. "You don't have to do this. We can find another way to get Reardon."

He stared down at her. "I thought this is what you wanted, Grace." To catch Reardon at any price. And after that—what was it she'd told him that first night? She didn't give a damn what happened to Ethan.

Her eyes were very blue and very mysterious in the candlelight. Ethan couldn't quite define the emotion he saw simmering just beneath the surface, but the possibilities tightened the nerves in his stomach.

"Just be careful," she murmured. Then she turned and walked away.

GRACE SAT AT a table near the back of the mirrored ballroom with a group of doctors and hospital administrators. She absently listened to the conversation around her as she scanned the crowded hall, looking, not just for Reardon, but for the agents she knew Myra would have in place tonight.

As for Myra, Grace had spotted her earlier, looking wonderful in a black sequined gown that would probably cause Vince Connelly, their section chief back in Washington, to have a heart attack when he got her expense account.

Grace didn't know where Myra was seated, but as her gaze continued to scour the room, someone else caught her attention. Pilar, on Bob Kendall's arm, made an entrance that could only be called spectacular. Dressed in a strapless red evening gown, Ethan's ex-wife had every male head in the room turning to stare at her admiringly.

The man beside Grace muttered something she couldn't understand. He'd introduced himself earlier as an administrator at a local hospital, and Grace had told him that she was a "friend of a friend" who had wangled an invitation for the event.

She turned to him now and asked, "I'm sorry. What did you say?"

He shrugged and lifted his champagne glass to his lips. "Pilar Hunter and Robert Kendall are the last two people I'd expect to see at an event honoring Ethan Hunter."

"Do you know them?" Grace tried to act no more than mildly curious.

"Only by reputation," the man said. "And rumor."

"Rumor?"

"Bob Kendall used to be Ethan's business partner. The two of them started a practice right after completing their residency. After a while, Ethan became somewhat of a celebrity. He started believing his own press and decided he no longer needed a partner. Most of the assets were in his name, and he had the hot reputation. Kendall had been content to work in the background and let Ethan have all the glory, but when Kendall was forced to go it alone, he discovered that most of his patients weren't willing to follow him. He was all but ruined. It's taken him a long time to even come close to where he was before.''

Grace listened to the story with interest. "So what is Dr. Kendall's connection with Pilar?"

The man beside her smiled knowingly. "I suspect she's become his consolation prize. And not a bad one at that, I must say.''

FROM HIS PLACE on the dais, Ethan examined the crowd, wondering how many of his enemies had bothered to show up tonight. Or should he say, Ethan Hunter's enemies?

What would the people in the audience say if he stood up suddenly and proclaimed that he wasn't who they thought he was? That he, in fact, had no idea who he was.

But even if he really *was* Ethan Hunter, he was still a fraud. A doctor who used the cover of his good deeds in order to take blood money from criminals. A man willing to risk everything for the sake of greed.

Ethan let his gaze move to Grace. She sat near the back of the room, but he could see her face in the candlelight. She was talking with the man seated to her right, and for a moment, Ethan felt a terrible envy well up inside him. He wanted to be the man near her. He wanted to be the one draping his arm across the back of her chair so that he could lean toward her and talk to her in low tones that no one else could hear.

He wanted to whisper things to her that he'd never told anyone else.

But how could he be sure he hadn't? How could he know how many women had come before her? How many he'd claimed to love?

Ethan stared at her, letting a dozen different emotions wash over him. He told himself he had no right to feel that way about her, because if he was Ethan Hunter, he didn't want to drag her down with him. And if he was someone else...someone who had been pursued through the jungle by the Mexican authorities...

He stopped himself, not wanting to dwell on the mysteries hidden somewhere in his mind. Not wanting to consider how, if he wasn't Ethan Hunter, he had come to have the man's face.

But whoever the hell he was, Grace Donovan should remain off limits, he thought gloomily, even though he knew she was no innocent in all this. Earlier, when he'd left her to take his place on the dais, he'd turned to see her talking to a woman in a black evening gown. The conversation had been brief and by all appearances casual, two women bumping into each other and then lingering for a moment to make small talk, to perhaps compliment one another on their gowns.

But Ethan had sensed something else was going on. An uneasiness had come over him as he stood watching them. Then the older one had looked up and caught his eye. She'd smiled briefly, as if acknowledging his interest, before saying something to Grace. The two women parted, and Grace hadn't looked back as she'd walked across the room to find her table. But Ethan was almost certain the dark-haired woman had said something to Grace about him, and that she'd known he was watching her.

Now, as she sat talking to the man beside her, she seemed just as determined to avoid Ethan's stare. He watched her for a long time, all through dinner and afterward, until, with something of a start, he heard his name being called. He looked up to find that a man had taken the podium. He introduced himself as Dr. Frank Melburne, then proceeded to introduce to the audience everyone else on the dais.

The names were a jumble to Ethan. He didn't bother to memorize them as he surveyed the crowded room, searching for the face of a killer.

Melburne spoke for several minutes, elaborating on the need for a new children's wing at St. Mary's, and how Ethan's work with underprivileged children, both here and in Mexico, should be an inspiration to all of them. He held up the framed citation that was being presented to Ethan, then concluded by saying, "And now I'd like to present the man of the hour, Dr. Ethan Hunter. Ethan?"

Ethan got up and walked to the microphone. He had anticipated being asked to say something tonight, but he hadn't prepared a speech. What the hell was he supposed to say? He didn't remember any of his deeds, good or bad. He didn't even know who he was—only that he was a man hunted by a killer.

Ethan stood at the podium, gazing out at the audience. Here I am, Reardon, he thought. *Where the hell are you?*

"I'm very honored to be here tonight," he finally said, his gaze lingering for one split second on Grace. "But what if I were to tell all of you that I'm not the man you think I am?"

WHAT IS HE DOING? Grace wondered uneasily. She watched Ethan from a distance, realizing that if Reardon were going to make a move tonight, it would be now. Ethan was an open target, and Reardon would relish an audience. She tensed, her gaze darting around the room as she fingered the gold clasp of her evening bag.

From the podium, Ethan said, "I'm not the man you think I am because I don't deserve this award. I'm sure there are any number of my colleagues here tonight who are much more deserving than I."

"What a surprise," the man beside Grace muttered. "Humility is not something one expects from Ethan Hunter."

Grace ignored the comment, focusing her attention on the room instead, watching for any sudden move, for anyone who looked the least bit suspect. A rustle near the center of the room drew her attention, but for a moment, she couldn't tell what was going on. Then Pilar, her red dress glowing like a beacon, stood and lifted her champagne glass toward the dais.

"False modesty doesn't become you, Ethan." Her clear, lyrical voice rang out over the ballroom. "Why don't you say what you really think about all these people? What you've told me dozens of times in the past? There's not a man or woman in this room—" she swung her glass around, sloshing champagne over the rim "—who can touch your skill as a surgeon. What do you call all of them? Oh, yes. Meat cutters. But you…you're different, aren't you, Ethan? A genius who can change a mortal woman into a goddess. I'm proof of that, aren't I?"

She stood in the center of the room, spreading her arms as if inviting the whole world to look upon her beauty, to worship it. She didn't appear to be carrying a weapon, but Grace slipped open her purse, her hand closing around the SIG-Sauer pistol.

Pilar slowly lowered her arms. "But what do you do

once you've created perfection? What is left then but to...destroy it?''

The room grew almost unbearably silent as everyone stared at Pilar. Grace found she couldn't tear her own gaze away. Something about the woman seemed almost...pathetic.

Out of the corner of Grace's eye, she could see Ethan still at the podium. He made no move to leave the dais or to silence his ex-wife. Like everyone else, his attention seemed to be riveted on her.

A man wearing a dark suit and an ear piece that immediately identified him as one of Myra's agents moved in toward Pilar. Before he could reached her, Bob Kendall jumped up and grabbed her arm. For a moment, the two of them almost scuffled, and then he said something to her that no one else could hear. Pilar resisted, then seemed to melt into Kendall. He put his arm around her and led her from the room.

Grace remained standing, adrenaline pumping through her veins. She combed the room, and saw Myra at the back near one of the colonnaded entrances, talking to Joe Huddleston, an agent Grace had known since Quantico. Huddleston turned and followed Pilar and Kendall out of the room. The agent who had been heading toward Pilar quietly faded into the background.

The room erupted into a cacophony of coughs and excited murmurs. Ethan remained at the podium. After a moment, he said, "Now that my fan club has left, we can get back to the business at hand."

Everyone remained stunned. Then there was a smattering of nervous laughter that took a few seconds to build. When everyone grew quiet again, the tension seemed to be somewhat relieved, and Ethan said with a shrug, "No matter what I say now, it's going to be anticlimactic, so let me just conclude by telling you how grateful—and how unworthy—I am to be receiving this honor.''

Dr. Melburne, who had been standing behind Ethan on the dais, took his cue. He stepped forward, handing the citation to Ethan and shaking his hand before quickly retreating into the background, as if not wanting to diminish the honoree's glory.

Ethan turned to say something to Melburne, then bent to retrieve a paper he'd knocked from the podium. For an instant, Melburne stood framed in the spotlight, his expression one of shock as his hand went to his chest.

When he brought his hand away, Grace could see his fingers were dripping with blood. A crimson bloom spread across the front of his shirt as he fell backward onto the stage.

Chapter Ten

When he saw Dr. Melburne fall, Ethan automatically went into a crouch as he whipped the gun from underneath his jacket. As the ballroom exploded in pandemonium, Ethan's gaze probed the room, trying to locate Grace, but it was impossible. People were screaming and mauling each other to get to the exits.

Gun still drawn, Ethan knelt beside Melburne and spread open the man's jacket. The entire front of his shirt was red, and blood gurgled from his mouth. Ethan glanced up at the row of stunned doctors on the dais. They seemed incapable of moving.

"Someone help this man," Ethan shouted. "Hurry!"

The command spurred them into action. Two of the doctors crawled along the dais to where Melburne lay and began working on him. Ethan saw one of the others barking orders into a cell phone, presumably calling 911.

Taking one last look at the fallen man, Ethan jumped from the dais into the mob scene on the main floor of the ballroom. He still couldn't see Grace, but he knew he had to find her before Reardon did. She could be in every bit as much danger as Ethan.

THE MOMENT GRACE saw the blood on Melburne's fingers, she drew her weapon. A woman at the table screamed while the man who sat next to Grace gazed at her in shock. "What the hell—"

"I'm a federal agent," Grace said. "All of you get down and stay down."

Whether they believed her or not, they didn't hesitate to follow her orders. They all hit the floor, scrambling for a position beneath the table.

Grace glanced around. The room was in chaos as men and women either tried to flee or were scuttling beneath the tables. She couldn't locate Myra, Huddleston or any of the other agents. Turning back to the dais, she saw Ethan leap to the floor and then plunge into the terrified throng.

What the hell was he doing? He should be trying to find cover. That bullet had been meant for him. If he hadn't bent to retrieve the paper—

Grace shuddered. Weapon at her side, she started through the crowd toward the dais. The majority of the exodus was taking place at the back, where the colonnaded exits were located. Grace made her way to one side, hugging the wall as she tried to catch another glimpse of Ethan. If he'd been hit… If she had let him get hit…

To Grace's right, a closed door was skillfully hidden between two of the mirrors. Until she was almost upon it, the door looked like one of the intricately carved wall panels. Cautiously, Grace opened the panel and glanced down a long corridor. It appeared to be some sort of service hall with swinging doors that led to the kitchen and work areas.

Near one end of the corridor, a man in a white

waiter's uniform cowered in a corner, his hands still clutching a circular tray of dirty dishes.

Grace started toward him. "I'm a federal agent," she said. "Don't move."

The man's expression was one of shock. He muttered something she couldn't understand. As Grace neared him, she saw that he was a middle-aged Hispanic with a swarthy complexion and dark, piercing eyes. A thin, black mustache traced the line of his upper lip, and a tiny gold hoop glinted from his left earlobe.

His eyes were wide with fright, and his hands trembled so badly, the crystal and cutlery made a jingling sound on the tray.

"Don't shoot, *por favor*." His tone was pleading, his voice heavily accented as he stared at the gun in Grace's hand.

She took another step toward him. "Just stay calm," she advised. "*¿Habla usted inglés?*"

"*Sí. Un poquito.*"

"Are you alone here? Have you seen anyone else in this hallway?"

His dark eyes lifted to hers. He nodded.

"Where? *¿Dónde?*"

He pointed down the hallway behind her. Grace glanced over her shoulder.

She sensed more than saw the man move toward her. She whirled back around, but as she did so, he slammed the tray into her stomach as hard as he could. The breath flew from her lungs, and Grace stumbled backward, falling against the wall and sliding to the floor. The man took off running toward the end of the hallway. He looked back only once before disappearing around a corner, but in that split second, Grace could have sworn she saw recognition flash across his features.

"Stop!" she commanded, but her gun had slipped out of her hand when she fell. She scrambled toward it, but the man was gone.

Fighting for breath, Grace pulled herself up from the floor and started after him. The adrenaline rushing through her veins was almost like a drug high. Her head spun dizzily, but she didn't hesitate.

Why had he run from her?

The most logical explanation was that he was an illegal alien who didn't want to be deported, but as Grace rounded the corner where she had last seen him, another thought came to her.

If he was nothing more than an illegal alien, why had she glimpsed a look of recognition on his face?

BY THIS TIME, hotel security had descended on the uproar in the ballroom. HPD would be close behind, and Ethan decided it probably wasn't a good idea to be seen with a loaded gun. He slipped the weapon beneath his jacket, into the waistband of his pants, as he hunted through the crowd. Where the hell was Grace?

Out of the corner of his eye, he caught a flash of midnight-blue, but when he turned, all he saw was his own reflection in one of the mirrors lining the side wall of the ballroom. Then one of the panels in the wall moved, and he realized it was a door that someone had just gone through. Ethan started across the room.

It seemed to take forever to tear his way through the hysterical crowd, but Ethan finally reached the side of the ballroom and located the door. He opened it and peered cautiously inside. Broken crystal and china lay strewn on the floor where a tray had been dropped.

Ethan started to back out of the hall, but then he noticed something else on the floor. An earring sparkling among the shards of broken glass. Grace's earring.

Drawing his gun, Ethan listened for a moment, then started down the corridor toward the sound of a closing door.

GRACE SHOVED OPEN a swinging door, and stepped into a damp, humid room with dim lighting.

The area was cavernous and eerie in its silence. Laundry bags hung from an overhead conveyor, and she stood motionless, searching for movement, the telltale swing of one of the bags as someone brushed by it.

Nothing moved. There wasn't so much as a whisper of sound.

As silently as she could, Grace reached down and removed her high heels. Then in stocking feet, she moved along the rows of laundry bags, searching for Reardon.

As she neared the end of one of the long aisles, the hair on the back of her neck rose. A breath of air touched her skin, as if someone had moved behind her.

Heart racing, Grace spun.

FOR A LONG moment, they stood staring at each other. Neither of them lowered their weapons as they faced off. Grace's gaze went to the gun in his hand, and one brow lifted ever so slightly. Then she raised a finger to her lips, warning Ethan to be silent. She motioned for him to take the right side of the room while she turned to search the left.

He hesitated. Something told him he wasn't used to

following orders, that he was the one who was usually in control of a situation like this. But under the circumstances, he couldn't find fault with Grace's logic. Split up. Circle the room. Force Reardon, or whomever she had cornered, out into the open.

Ethan made his way through the mountain of laundry bags stacked in bins along the side of the room. There were any number of hiding places, and flushing out their quarry might not be so easy. But just as the thought occurred to him, Ethan caught sight of something in one of the bins. A flash of black among all the white linen.

He eased forward, until he was directly in front of the bin. The black he'd seen was the arm of someone's tuxedo jacket, but he didn't think it belonged to Reardon. Someone was still wearing the jacket, and a crimson stain was spreading slowly over the soiled laundry hiding the body.

Silently, Ethan unearthed the victim. He didn't recognize the man, but he knew the ear piece the man still wore indicated a cop of some kind. Obviously, he and Grace weren't the only ones on Reardon's trail.

He wondered who the victim was, but he didn't take time to search for his ID. The bullet hole through the man's neck was enough for Ethan.

He had to find Grace.

THE ECHO OF her heartbeat sounded deafening to Grace. She wondered if Reardon could hear it. Wondered if he was taking pleasure from it.

The damp humidity in the laundry room was almost stifling. Grace found she had a hard time breathing. Sweat trickled down the side of her face, but she didn't waste a motion on swiping it away. She couldn't let down her guard for even a second.

At the far end of the room, away from the entrance where she'd come in, a sound finally came to Grace. At first, she wondered if it might be Ethan, but then as she stood listening, she identified the creak and rumble of an elevator car sliding down the cable.

Grace whirled and took off toward the sound. She didn't bother now to try and conceal her movements. If Reardon made it inside the elevator before she could get to him—

She fought her way out of the suspended laundry bags just in time to see the heavy metal doors sliding closed. Grace lunged toward the elevator, jamming the button with the heel of her hand so hard, pain ripped all the way up to her elbow. Ignoring the pain, she tried to pry open the doors, but it was no use. The car began to ascend.

ETHAN EMERGED from the forest of laundry in time to see Grace pound the elevator door in frustration. When she heard him approach, she looked around, wild-eyed and desperate.

"The stairs," she said hoarsely. "Come on. We have to find him."

She didn't wait to see if Ethan followed her, but turned and raced through the door, retracing their steps down the corridor to a door marked Stairs.

He wondered why he didn't try to reason with her, why he didn't try to stop her from pursuing a cold-blooded killer. She was in danger, but it never occurred to Ethan to grab Grace and hold her back. She was too competent. Too coldly determined, and besides. She had a gun. If he tried to stop her now, she might just use it on him.

Ethan caught her on the stairs and overtook her. She wouldn't care for that, he thought fleetingly, but he was still a man, still had enough of the protective instinct to want to go first and blaze the trail. If he couldn't take out Trevor Reardon, Ethan could at least do enough damage so that Grace would have a chance.

They burst through the stairwell door on the second level. Two uniformed maids stood in the hallway chatting beside their carts. They looked up in surprise and then in terror when they saw the weapons.

"The service elevator," Ethan said. "Where is it?"

Neither of them said anything, but one of them pointed to the far end of the corridor. Grace darted past Ethan, and he swore, wishing she'd stay behind him.

They were only halfway down the hall when they heard the elevator doors swish open. Grace gasped in dismay and lunged forward, throwing herself at the elevator and managing just barely to get her fingers between the doors.

Ethan put his hands above hers, and as the doors yielded to their pressure, both Grace and Ethan jumped back and raised their weapons.

The doors slid open, but the car was empty except for a white, blood-stained waiter's coat lying on the floor.

GRACE SPUN, HER gaze frantically searching the hall. But she knew Reardon hadn't gotten off on this floor because he'd never been in the elevator to begin with. She'd let herself fall for the oldest trick in the book.

She whirled back to the elevator and started to step inside, but Ethan caught her arm. She flung off his hand. "What are you doing? He's still in the laundry. We have to get back down there."

Ethan put away his gun. "He's gone, Grace."

"You don't know that," she said angrily. "He may still be down there. You don't have to come with me, but I'm going back. I'll search every inch of that place, look in every laundry bag down there if I have to, but I'll find him. He won't get away. I won't let him—" She stopped herself as she realized how she must sound to Ethan. How she must look. Like a woman completely out of control.

And that's exactly how she felt. Reardon had thwarted her again. Made her act without thinking.

Grace forced herself to step out of the elevator, to take a long, deep breath. Ethan was still staring down at her, and the look on his face was not one Grace thought she could easily forget. His eyes were dark and narrowed, his mouth set in a grim, forbidding line. She found herself shivering and wondering about the outcome when and if Ethan Hunter and Trevor Reardon ever came face to face.

Ethan wasn't like any doctor she'd ever known before, that was for damn sure.

She said almost calmly, "Where did you get the gun?"

He shrugged, but his gaze darkened. "I found it in the safe at the house. I thought it might be useful tonight."

Grace was tempted to give him the old lecture about weapons in the hands of amateurs, but she was suddenly too weary. And besides, she had a feeling Ethan Hunter could handle a gun as effectively as he could wield a scalpel. She was the last person to underestimate him.

She slipped her own gun back inside her purse. "I guess you're right. Reardon's probably long gone by now."

"He left a calling card in the laundry," Ethan said. "Or at least someone did. There's a man with a bullet through his neck down there. I think he's a cop."

"My God," Grace whispered. Was he one of Myra's agents? Someone Grace knew?

She turned back to the elevator. "We'd better get back down there. Maybe you can help him."

Ethan caught her arm. "Nobody can help him, Grace. He's dead."

She hesitated. "We still have to call someone. We can't just leave him down there."

"I know exactly what we have to do."

Grace glanced up at him. Something in his voice alarmed her. "What do you mean?"

Ethan's expression turned grim. "We were fools to think we could do this alone. Reardon is a killer. A master criminal who has escaped from prison twice. And now at least three people are dead because he's after me. First Amy, then Melburne, and now the man downstairs. How many more people have to die because of me?"

The guilt in his eyes was not an easy thing to witness. Grace said urgently, "This isn't your fault. You didn't kill those people."

"That's not what you said the first night I met you." His voice hardened with disgust. "You said I had a part in Amy's death. And if everything you suspect is true, you were right."

Grace stared helplessly at Ethan. She didn't know what to say to him.

He put his hands on her shoulders, gazing down into

her eyes. For the longest moment, they stayed that way as a myriad of emotions flashed across his face. Then he said, "I can't risk your life to save my own skin, Grace. I won't. I'm calling Pope and telling him everything. I'm going to end this tonight. I don't care what happens to me, but we have to get the police involved. Now."

His words blew Grace away. She couldn't believe he was willing to subject himself to a police investigation, to face a prison sentence in order to keep her safe from Reardon.

How long had it been since someone had cared about her that much? Since she had allowed anyone to care about her?

Until that moment, Grace hadn't realized just how lonely she'd been all these years. How empty her life had become.

Now that knowledge was almost like a physical ache inside her.

She closed her eyes briefly, making a decision that she knew might cost her everything. When she spoke, she heard her voice quiver with emotion. "You don't have to call anyone," she told Ethan. "I am the police."

Chapter Eleven

Back at Ethan's house, Grace stood at the second-story window, staring out. From her vantage, she could see over the brick wall surrounding the grounds to the street beyond where an unmarked car was parked at the curb. The neighborhood sparkled with lights, but the dark sedan blended into the shadows cast by the water oaks lining the sidewalk.

In the opposite direction, where two streets intersected and formed a tiny parklike area in the median, a man stood smoking in the dark. Grace could see the glowing tip of his cigarette lift and fall.

Though from this distance, she couldn't see his radio or his weapon, she knew he would have both, and that he would remain in constant communication with Myra and with the man in the car. After tonight, the operation had suddenly become personal to every agent and support personnel working the case. Joe Huddleston, a well-liked and respected agent assigned to the field office here in Houston, had been killed. Murdered in cold blood, his body stuffed down a laundry chute at the hotel like so much dirty linen.

Grace had known Joe for years. They'd gone through training together at Quantico. He was one of the few agents in the FBI who knew her entire story. And now he was dead. Because of Reardon.

For a moment, Grace's hatred threatened to consume her, but she forced herself to stand back, take a breath, look at everything logically. There would be time enough later to mourn Joe's death. For now, she had to remain focused.

Could she be absolutely sure that Reardon was responsible for Joe's death? Was Reardon the man she'd seen in the corridor of the hotel? If so, his disguise—whether temporary or permanent—had been nothing short of miraculous.

Grace's mind went back over the events of the evening. The last time she'd seen Huddleston was when he'd followed Pilar and Kendall out of the ballroom. Was it possible that Pilar's little scene had been a diversion? Was she or Kendall—or perhaps both of them—responsible for the shot that had been meant for Ethan tonight? Had they killed Joe Huddleston?

Grace knew that Myra had someone working on that angle even now, but the older agent was still concentrating most of her efforts on Reardon.

When Grace had contacted her earlier, before leaving the hotel, and told her what she planned to do, Myra had been against it. "You can't tell him the truth, Grace. What if he runs?"

"I don't think he will," Grace had argued. "And besides, I don't have a choice. If I don't tell him the truth, he's going to the police. The last thing we need is to get HPD involved any more than they already are."

She'd finally managed to placate Myra, but Grace knew Ethan wouldn't be quite as easy to appease. She wouldn't soon forget the look on his face when she'd told him she was the police. A federal agent, she'd barely managed to get out before the hotel security and several HPD officers had descended upon them in the corridor.

Grace wasn't sure why, but Ethan hadn't said anything to the authorities about what she'd told him. Instead, he'd let her take the lead, and when it had come time for him to give a statement, he hadn't said or done anything to give her away. That action, as much as anything else, made Grace realize how much he had come to trust her. How much she owed him.

And now it was time to pay the piper, she thought, turning away from the window. Ethan, who had gone straight to the kitchen to mix himself a drink when they'd gotten home, would want an explanation, and she had better be convincing. For more reasons than one.

Across the room, Simon moved restlessly on his perch. Grace drifted over to him and stood staring at him for a moment.

"What did you mean yesterday when you said, 'I say we just the kill the bastard and be done with it'?" she asked him.

The bird tilted his head and squawked, "They're not real."

"Forget about that," Grace said impatiently. "We're way beyond that now."

The bird strutted along his perch. "Book him, Dano!"

For God's sake, Grace thought. The bird was a walking, talking advertisement for daytime TV.

"Who do you think I am, Jack Lord?" she muttered.

"That's a good question," Ethan said. She turned to

find him standing behind her, a drink in each hand. "Who are you, Grace?"

She moistened her lips. "I told you earlier. I'm a federal agent."

"FBI."

She nodded. "That's right."

"Is your name really Grace Donovan?"

"Yes."

"And I'm supposed to believe this new story? Accept your word for everything?"

"I can show you my ID and my badge if you like."

"Don't bother. I'm sure they can be faked just like business cards. And sisters." He offered her one of the drinks. When Grace declined, he said bitterly, "Oh, that's right. You're still on the job, aren't you?"

"Look." She ran her fingers through her bangs, wondering how she could possibly explain her motives in a way that would make him understand. Make him forgive her. "I'm sorry I didn't tell you the truth from the start. But I couldn't. It wasn't my call to make."

His gaze narrowed on her. "So you were just following orders?"

She hesitated. It would be easy to blame everything on her superiors, but the truth was, the deception had been her idea. Hers and hers alone.

She drew a long breath and released it. "Maybe I should start from the first."

"Maybe you should," he agreed. He downed one of the drinks and set the empty glass aside before turning back to her. "I'm listening."

Grace turned and walked back to the windows that looked out upon the street. The surveillance was still in place, but she wondered why that knowledge didn't alleviate the uneasiness growing inside her. After she told Ethan the truth, would he allow her to stay? Would he accept her protection?

"Three days before Amy Cole was murdered, she walked into the Federal Building here in Houston and asked to speak to an FBI agent. She said it was urgent. The man she eventually talked to was Joe Huddleston."

She sensed rather than saw Ethan's surprise. "The agent who was killed tonight?"

Grace nodded. "Joe and I went through training at Quantico together. We'd kept in touch over the years. He knew that my superior in Washington was coordinating efforts to locate Trevor Reardon. After he talked to Amy, he got in touch with us immediately."

"What did Amy tell him?" Ethan came to stand beside her at the window.

"She said that her employer, Dr. Ethan Hunter, the renowned plastic surgeon, was using his clinic in Mexico to operate on criminals' faces for money."

"What proof did she offer?"

Grace paused. "None. All she had were suspicions."

He made a sudden, angry movement that startled Grace. "Are you telling me you have no proof that anything illegal went down? This whole thing has been based on one woman's suspicions?"

"I know how that must make you feel, but—"

"Oh, I don't think you do," he said coldly. "I don't think you have any idea how I feel at this moment."

"You have every right to be angry," Grace said, wishing his eyes didn't look quite so dark and quite so deadly. "But let me finish before you start jumping to conclusions yourself."

He let that one pass. He turned back and stared out the window with a brooding frown.

"Amy showed Joe Huddleston a picture she'd clipped from the newspaper of Trevor Reardon. It was the same one I showed you. She said that she was almost certain she'd seen Reardon talking with Dr. Hunter...with you...a few months ago at the Mexican clinic."

Ethan glanced at her, his gaze still hard. "Go on."

"Like I said before, Joe knew my superior, Myra Temple, was coordinating the Bureau's efforts to track down Reardon. After Amy left, he called me and told me what had happened. When I briefed Myra, she agreed that we needed to come down here and talk to Amy ourselves, see if her story held water. We didn't discount the possibility that she could have been delusional, or that she was a rejected mistress out for revenge. We wanted to consider every possibility.

"And after talking with her, both Myra and I believed her. We both thought she was on to something. Myra and I started working with the field office here in Houston to set up a surveillance and possibly a sting if it was necessary to get your cooperation."

He spared her a brief glance. "Just what were you willing to do to *get* my cooperation?"

Grace shrugged. "Whatever it took."

A look she couldn't define flashed across his face. "I accused you once of being cold, remember?"

"Yes. And you were right." She forced herself to shrug. "I am cold. Ruthless. I'll do whatever it takes to catch Trevor Reardon."

Ethan's gaze hardened on her. "Why does it mean so much to you?"

Grace tried to suppress a shudder. She wanted to be honest with Ethan, but there were some things she'd never told anyone. Some things she still couldn't talk about. "He's a killer. A cold-blooded murderer. I don't want anyone else to die because of him."

"And that's all it is?" Ethan's voice had a strange quality that Grace had never heard before.

She shivered again. "Isn't that enough?"

He fell silent for a moment, contemplating everything she'd told him. Then he said, "What went wrong? Why is Amy Cole dead?"

Grace released a long breath. "After talking with her, we didn't expect you back in the country for at least two weeks. We thought we had plenty of time to set everything up, get everyone in place so that no one would get hurt. But evidently Amy got cold feet. She may even have found out about your impending divorce and then had second thoughts about what she'd done to you.

"When she found out you were coming back early, I think she got in touch with you and warned you that the Feds would be waiting for you. We had the airport staked out, along with your house and Amy's apartment. We thought we had it all covered, at least as best we could with such short notice, but then you chartered a plane and flew into a private airfield. We think you somehow contacted Amy, either by cell phone or through a neighbor, and the two of you made plans to meet at the clinic, possibly to get rid of incriminating evidence. Amy somehow managed to slip through our surveillance, and then hours later, she turned up dead."

Grace glanced up and saw Ethan's reflection in the window. He was staring at her, and the look on his face...the expression in his eyes unnerved her.

"That still doesn't tell me what happened to her," he said slowly. "Unless you're implying that I killed her."

Grace spun toward him. "No, that's not what I think. That's not what any of us think. Trevor Reardon followed you, probably all the way from Mexico. He ambushed you at the clinic and made it look like you'd stumbled upon a robbery, an addict looking for drugs. I never thought you killed Amy," Grace repeated. Somehow she had to make him believe that. She had to at least give him that.

"How did you know to go to the clinic?" he asked.

Grace shrugged. "That was purely a hunch. What I told you before was true—I was supposed to meet Amy that night. When she didn't show and I found out she'd slipped out of her apartment unseen, I knew I had to find her. I knew she could be in danger. So I went to the clinic, almost as a last measure. When I found out what had happened, I knew I couldn't tell the police who I really was. The homicide was their jurisdiction, and if they found out Amy had been working with the FBI, we would have had to bring them in on the case. It would have tipped off Reardon that we were on to him, and so I told them I was Amy's sister."

Ethan cocked a dark brow, staring down at her. "You didn't think she might have a real sister who would come forward and dispute you?"

"I knew she didn't. She'd already told me she had no one, and that she didn't like to talk about her past. I felt the cover would be reasonably secure."

"And so then you decided to approach me." Ethan turned back to the window. "I still don't understand why you didn't tell me the truth. Wouldn't that have been simpler?"

"Maybe," Grace agreed. "But I couldn't take that chance. I had no reason to believe you'd be willing to cooperate. Why would you?"

"I don't know," he said flippantly. "To save my life, maybe? Because it would have been the decent thing to do?"

Grace said nothing.

After a moment, Ethan said, "I guess my amnesia was a bonus for you then."

She didn't bother to deny it. "It made you vulnerable. You couldn't go to the police without incriminating yourself. And without a memory, without knowing who wanted you dead, you couldn't protect yourself, either. I made sure you had to turn to me."

He winced at that. "Tell me something, Grace. How far were you willing to go to get my cooperation?"

"I already told you. Whatever was necessary."

"Did that include this?" He turned suddenly and grabbed her shoulders, forcing her to face him. His eyes were dark and turbulent, his expression like an icy mask. When he kissed her, Grace's first instinct was to push him away, to somehow try and regain control of the situation.

But a split second later, she felt the ice inside him begin to melt. She knew, instinctively, what he wanted at that moment. What he needed.

She kissed him back with every ounce of her strength. With every fiber of her being. With every emotion that raged through her mind and body and soul.

When he finally pulled away, they both stood shaken by the experience. Grace's knees trembled weakly, but she forced herself to remain steady, to stare up at him as openly and honestly as she dared.

"That was never a lie," she finally whispered. "The way I feel about you is something I never counted on."

His hands were still on her shoulders. He stared

down at her for a long time, his breathing ragged. "How do you feel?"

Grace's heart pounded against her chest. It had been a long time since she'd had a conversation like this. Since she had felt this exposed. "It's like you said once. We're connected somehow. I don't understand it, but…it's more than just attraction. It's as if…"

"We're meant for each other," he said.

Grace closed her eyes. "But I *can't* feel that way. I can't let my emotions get in my way. I can't forget who I am or what I have to do. And I can't forget who you are, either."

"Who I am." His hands dropped from her shoulders and he turned and walked away from her.

Grace hesitated, unsure whether or not to follow him. But he didn't go far. He walked to the center of the room and stood looking around, as if he suddenly realized he didn't belong there.

For a long moment, neither of them said anything, then he turned to her. His gaze was shadowed with an emotion that made Grace's breath quicken. "I'm not the man you think I am."

"You've said that before." She moved across the room toward him. "And I think I understand why you feel that way. It's like there're two sides of you. One man operates on criminals' faces for money, while the other can change monsters into angels. That man can give children without hope a whole new life. That's the man you really are, Ethan. That's the man you remember. The other one doesn't seem real to you because you don't want to be him."

Uncertainty flickered in his eyes. Then his gaze darkened again. "That's a rather whimsical explanation for an FBI agent, Grace. I don't think you buy it any more than I do.''

"You're wrong. I do believe it." On impulse, Grace put a hand on his sleeve, felt him tense at her touch. "I know there's something fine and decent about you. I know there's goodness in you, just like there's darkness." She paused, searching for the right words. "Who knows what brings that darkness to the surface, but I think we all have the capacity for it. I think there's darkness in all of us."

His brow lifted at that. "Even you?"

She gave a bitter little laugh. "Maybe even especially me. I'm not sure I'm in any position to judge you, no matter what you've done."

He didn't seem to hear her. He'd turned away and walked back over to the window to stare out. After a bit, he said, "It's been a long day and I'm beat. We can talk about this in the morning, decide what to do then."

Grace had brought a bag over earlier before they'd gone to the Huntington, but after her confession, she wasn't sure he'd let her stay. But it appeared now that he'd accepted her presence, and for the time being at least, wasn't going to ask her to leave. Grace was glad. She would hate to have to force the issue now.

"That's probably a good idea," she agreed. "We could both use some rest. I'll see you in the morning."

She waited for him to turn and acknowledge her leaving, but he remained at the window, his back to her. He didn't even say good-night, and after a moment, Grace turned and left the room.

A FEDERAL AGENT. A COP.

Ethan should have known. And maybe a part of him

had known. He couldn't say her revelation had come as that much of a shock. He'd always known there was something Grace wasn't telling him. That there was more to her than a grieving sister.

No wonder she had seemed so confident in her ability to deal with Trevor Reardon. She was trained to deal with the likes of him.

Ethan thought about that for a moment. How did that make him feel? he wondered. Knowing that Grace was an agent who had not only been sent here to find Reardon, but to also protect Ethan in the process. How did he feel about his life being put in a woman's hands? In Grace's hands?

He tried to muster up the requisite resentment, but it wasn't in him. There were too many other things about the situation that troubled him more. The fact that she had lied to him, deceived him into believing she was Amy's sister. The fact that those lies had seemed so easy for Grace.

He'd been a means to an end for her. It was as simple as that.

Oh, he knew she was attracted to him. She couldn't hide it and she hadn't bothered to deny it. But her desire to find Trevor Reardon far exceeded her desire for Ethan, and that fact bothered him the most. She was a consummate professional before she was a woman, and Ethan knew that situation wasn't likely to change any time soon. At least not for him.

He remembered the way her eyes had burned with an inner fire when she'd first told him about Reardon, and an uneasiness Ethan couldn't explain swept over him.

What was it about Reardon that made Grace so passionate in her hatred of him, that made her almost careless in her pursuit of him?

What had made this assignment so personal for her?

Ethan knew the answer even before the question had completely formed in his mind, and a sick feeling rose in his throat as he stood staring out into the darkness.

GRACE STOOD WRAPPED in a towel at the bathroom mirror as she blow-dried her short hair. Afterward, she gazed at her reflection for a long time, wondering if she had done the right thing by telling Ethan as much as she had. But she hadn't really had a choice. Once he'd decided to go to the police with the story, she'd had to tell him the truth, and trust that he would continue to cooperate with her.

But why should he? She'd lied to him, deceived him at every possible turn. Why would he want anything more to do with her?

The end may have justified the means, but right now, Grace was having a hard time dealing with her conscience. She had deliberately put Ethan's life on the line in order to capture Reardon, and she hadn't even had the decency to tell him why. At least not completely.

Her past was something Grace had never told anyone. She couldn't even talk about it with Myra. What Trevor Reardon had done to her and her family was too personal, and Grace had never gotten over the guilt, let alone the shame.

She hadn't told Ethan because she hadn't wanted to see the disgust in his eyes over what she had done.

Grace didn't want to see it in her own eyes, either. She turned away from the mirror and walked into the guest bedroom where she'd left her suitcase earlier.

Digging through the contents, she pulled out a pair of white silk pajamas and put them on. As she was turning down the bed, the door behind her opened.

Grace grabbed her gun from the top of the nightstand, going instantly into a crouch while, with a two-handed grip, she swung the weapon toward the door.

Ethan stood just inside the room, his gaze going first to the gun in her hand, then to her face. He wore jeans, no shirt, and his dark hair glinted with moisture, as if he'd just come from the shower. Grace's hand trembled on the weapon as she stared at him, her awareness of him surging over her in a crest of heat.

As he walked into the room, she hesitated, then slowly lowered the weapon. She placed it on the nightstand behind her.

Ethan came over and stood in front of her. He didn't touch her, but his nearness made Grace's breath quicken. The look on his face made her heart pound inside her. She was tempted to put her hands on his bare chest, to feel the hardness beneath her fingers.

"You're her, aren't you?"

Grace stared up at him as a shock wave rolled over her. "What are you talking about?"

"The FBI agent's daughter you told me about. The only one in his family who didn't get killed in the fire. The one Trevor Reardon came back for. You're her."

She turned away, but he put his hands on her arms, forcing her to face him. She didn't want to. She didn't want to see the look in his eyes.

"Why didn't you tell me?" he demanded.

"I couldn't. After all these years, it's still too...painful." And she still couldn't look at him.

He put one hand under her chin, tilting her head up so that she had no choice but to meet his gaze. What she saw in his eyes wasn't disgust. It was another emotion that took Grace's breath away.

"What happened that night?" he asked softly.

"Please." Her eyes closed briefly. "I can't talk about it. I've never talked about it."

"Don't you think it's time you did?"

"It's too personal." She put trembling fingertips to her lips. "I don't think I *can* tell you. I don't think I want you to know."

"You said earlier that you weren't in any position to judge me. That goes both ways, Grace."

When she looked up at him, his eyes were so dark and so haunted, she thought for a moment she was staring at her own reflection. She took a step back from him, and he let her go.

He walked to the window to stare out into the darkness. "I think I may be exactly the person you need to talk to." There was something about his voice that was different.

Grace shivered, staring as his profile. After a moment, she said, "My father was the agent who arrested Reardon. The FBI had been after him for a long time, years. After he left the military, he became a killer for hire, an assassin at first, taking out government officials in foreign countries and certain high-powered businessmen for money. Then he fell in with some zealots in the Middle East and discovered they were willing to pay big bucks to someone with his expertise to carry out their dirty work. The notoriety appealed to Reardon, as did the money. And the killings."

She paused, trying to get her thoughts in order. Trying to dispel the tormented images twisting and turning in her mind. "My father tracked him for over two years and was finally able to arrest him. But before Reardon could stand trial, he escaped. I'd heard my father mention his name at the time of the arrest, but he never told us about Reardon's escape. I guess he didn't want to worry us, and I don't think he really believed Reardon would come after him. He thought Reardon would flee the country, but my father underestimated Reardon's obsession with order, with tying up loose ends.''

Ethan glanced at her then, but he still said nothing.

Grace took a long breath and continued. "He got into our house one day when everyone was gone and planted a bomb. He rigged all the doors and windows with explosive devices that were wired in to the main timer. When he detonated the bomb, the other devices were then triggered to explode if anyone tried to open the doors or windows from the inside or the out. It was an unbelievably intricate design and one he'd used before, on an Italian businessman's home several years before that. When the bomb exploded, the whole house erupted into flames. My mother and father were on the ground level, but my sister was trapped upstairs. I saw her at the window. Her hair and clothes were on fire—''

Grace broke off abruptly as the images bombarded her. Ethan had turned to face her, but he didn't move toward her. "I can't imagine what that must have been like for you.''

Grace shrugged. "No one can. I arrived right after the first bomb exploded, but the fire spread so fast, they didn't have a chance. The booby-trapped doors and windows were almost overkill.''

"Where were you?'' Ethan finally asked. It was the question Grace had been dreading.

She squeezed her eyes shut as if she could somehow stop the screams inside her head. "I was with him. I was with Trevor Reardon.'' She put her hands to her face and turned her back to Ethan.

The room was so quiet, Grace could hear the blood pounding in her ears. She sensed Ethan's shock, the deep revulsion he must feel for what she'd just told him.

After a moment of stunned silence, she felt his hands on her wrists, pulling her hands away from her face. ''Tell me the rest,'' he commanded softly.

Grace shuddered. ''I'd met him a few days before the fire. I realized afterward that he'd sought me out. It was all part of his game, the ultimate way to get back at my father, and I was so gullible. So *stupid*. I fell for everything he told me because I wanted to believe an older, sophisticated man could find me special and desirable. He seduced me,'' she said, trying to swallow past the nausea that rose in her throat. ''But I let him. I *wanted* it.''

When she would have turned away, Ethan clung to her hands. ''How old were you?''

''Old enough to know better.''

''How old?''

She drew a long breath. ''Seventeen.''

''You were a kid, Grace. You were no match for Reardon.''

''But I should have known,'' she said in anguish. ''I should have known who he was, what he planned to do. I should have been able to stop him.''

A tear slid down her face, the drop of moisture as foreign to her as the look of compassion in Ethan's eyes. Releasing one of her hands, he wiped the tear away with his fingertip, the gesture so gentle and so caring that Grace felt more tears, deeper tears rising inside her. With sheer force of will, she blinked them back.

"You've carried this guilt inside you all these years," Ethan said, staring down at her. "Don't you think it's time to let it go? Don't you think it's time to forgive yourself for having once been young and naive?"

"I didn't just go out and skip school," she said almost angrily. "I didn't stay out past my curfew. My whole family was killed while I—"

"There was nothing you could have done to stop Reardon. Deep down inside, you have to know that. He would have done what he did whether you had been with him or not. The only difference was, you stayed alive. And I think that's what you haven't been able to forgive yourself for."

Grace bowed her head, overcome with emotion. She couldn't say a word, couldn't deny or acknowledge what he was saying. All she could do was let him reach for her gently and draw her into the warm circle of his arms.

A part of her wanted to resist, because she knew she was vulnerable tonight in a way she hadn't been in years. She needed Ethan's arms around her more desperately than she would ever have thought possible. And that scared her. Terrified her.

Neither of them said anything for a very long time. They stood motionless, Ethan's arms around her while Grace battled the demons inside her that had threatened to destroy her for years.

After a while, the demons didn't seem quite so powerful. The images inside her mind weren't quite so strong. Grace lifted her face to Ethan's. "I've never told anyone what happened back then. There are those in the Bureau who know. Myra Temple, the woman who saved my life when Reardon came back for me, and Joe Huddleston. A few others who knew because they were around when it happened. But I've never been able to tell anyone else. I've never trusted anyone enough.''

Something flashed in Ethan's eyes, an emotion so dark, Grace shivered. "I hope you've done the right thing telling me."

She pulled back a little to stare up at him. "I don't understand."

He hesitated. "I hope I'm worthy of your trust."

Grace knew instantly what he meant. He was no longer thinking about what she'd told him, but about his own past. About the things he'd done. The demons he now had to battle.

She reached up and touched his face with her fingertips. "I meant what I said earlier. I know there's goodness in you. And now you know about the darkness in me. Does it change the way you feel?"

He almost smiled at that. "If anything, it only strengthens the bond between us. It makes me want you even more."

The fire in his eyes was suddenly an emotion Grace did recognize. Passion. The powerful kind. The reckless kind. The kind that matched the slow heat building inside her.

With a sense of inevitability that was almost stunning, Grace watched as he lowered his head toward hers. Their gazes clung for a long, scorching moment before his lips touched hers. Grace's eyes drifted closed as a shudder ripped through her. Ethan's kiss was powerful, electric, breathtaking. An explosion of desire that made her knees grow weak and her heartbeat thunder.

This was not attraction, she thought weakly. This was not chemistry. This was…destiny. This was a moment that had to be, no matter what the consequences.

She wrapped her arms around his neck and threaded her fingers through his hair. Ethan's own hands splayed against her back, holding her closely for a moment before starting to move over her in slow, deliberate strokes. Her back, her hips, her breasts, and then upward to cup her face. He broke the kiss to whisper against her mouth, "God, Grace…"

She couldn't have put it more eloquently herself. She pulled him to her, kissing him with an urgency that left them both gasping for breath. He pushed her back on the bed and moved over her, his fingers ripping loose the buttons on her pajamas so they could lay skin to skin. Heartbeat to heartbeat.

Grace shivered as his body molded to hers, as his mouth ground into hers. She accepted the assault, welcomed it. Wanted more of it.

They rolled over, and Grace was suddenly on top, staring down at him. His eyes were heavy-lidded and seductive, his mouth a sensuous invitation. She kissed the scar above his brow, his temple, then skimmed along the side of his face to tease his earlobe with her tongue.

He groaned and shuddered as she pressed her body into his and moved against him. After a few moments, he rolled them again, and now he was back on top, back in charge, and Grace was pliant beneath him. And then he did to her exactly what she had done to him.

The teasing became almost unbearable. The buildup almost the release. Grace's fingers moved to the buttons at the front of his jeans, but to her surprise, his hand closed over hers, stopping her.

His lips hovered over hers, a breathless heartbeat away. Then he lifted himself, so that for a moment they were staring into each other's eyes. His gaze was still clouded with passion, intense with longing, but another emotion simmered just beneath the surface. An emotion that made Grace almost gasp when she saw it.

Regret. Maybe even guilt.

She lay staring up at him, helpless with her own desire.

"I can't do this," he said.

A rush of humiliation swept over her. "What?"

He lifted himself off her and sat on the edge of the bed, his back to her. He put his hands to his face and scrubbed. "I can't do this to you."

Grace sat up, too, wrapping her pajama top around her and drawing her knees up to her chest. She rested her cheek on her knees, saying nothing. Embarrassment heated her skin, but it was a remorse that wasn't pure because even in the face of rejection, she still wanted him. Her body still quivered with need.

"I told you before that I'm not the man you think I am." He turned his head slightly, so that she could see a little of his profile. "I deliberately let you misunderstand what I meant. You think there're two sides to my personality—a good one and a dark one. And now that I've lost my memory, the good one is winning out. But you're wrong, Grace. Dead wrong."

He turned on the bed to face her, and Grace lifted her head to stare at him. "What do you mean?"

"I'm not Ethan Hunter."

Grace sat up, forgetting about the torn-away buttons on her top. The silk parted, and for just an instant, she saw Ethan's gaze waver. Then he glanced away, running a hand through his dark hair. "I'm not Dr. Ethan Hunter," he repeated.

Grace said breathlessly, "If you're not Ethan Hunter, then who are you?"

He shrugged. "I don't know. I don't even know *what* I am. What I may have done. When I woke up in the hospital a few days ago, the only thing I could remember at first was running through the jungle, being pursued by men with guns. Those men were the Mexican police, and they shot me. Here." He touched a spot on his side hidden by his jeans. "I fell from a cliff. When I came to in the hospital and found out who I was—or who I thought I was—I convinced myself that the whole episode was just a dream. The scar on my side was from the appendectomy I'd supposedly had recently. And everything else started to fall into place. I remembered then that I'd been in a clinic, that a man wearing a ski mask had been standing over me with a gun. I remembered Amy walking in, and then the fight I had with the gunman. He knocked me unconscious, and I assumed that's how I got the amnesia."

Grace stared at him in shock, not knowing where he was going with his story, but sensing it might be a place she didn't want to follow. "That's what everyone assumed. I don't understand, Ethan. Why do you think you're not Dr. Hunter?"

"Because I don't think the skills of a surgeon, especially one as talented as I'm supposed to be, would be something I would forget."

Grace frowned. "You can't know that for sure."

"Then how do you explain the other things that I didn't forget. Like how to use a weapon." To demonstrate his point, he picked up Grace's gun from the nightstand, ejected the clip, pulled back the slide to remove the bullet from the chamber, and then slammed home the magazine once again. He stared at the weapon for a moment, then laid it aside with a visible shudder.

"A lot of people know how to use a gun."

He stared at her. "So you're saying you don't think it's strange that I remember how to do what I just did with your gun, but I wouldn't have the faintest idea what to do with a scalpel if you handed me one right now."

Grace shrugged. "Amnesia is a tricky thing. I'm just saying that from what you've told me so far—"

"There's more," he said darkly. He got up and started to pace the room. "The man I dream about in the jungle—I know his fear. I know he's me. But his face isn't the one I see when I look in the mirror."

A cold chill slipped over Grace. "But maybe it is just a dream."

"Maybe. But how do you explain the fact that there are dozens of pairs of shoes in my closet, and not a single one fits me. They're all too small by at least half a size."

Grace couldn't explain that. The chill inside her deepened. "Are you sure? You tried them all on?"

"Every last one of them. The clothes aren't a perfect fit, either, but I attributed that to a weight loss following surgery. But I can't explain the shoes. Can you?"

Grace wrapped her pajama top more tightly around her. "There has to be a logical explanation."

"And then there's the gun," Ethan said, as if he hadn't heard her. "I found the pistol you saw earlier in the safe downstairs. I knew the moment I saw it that the gun belonged to me. I knew exactly what it would feel like to shoot it, the accuracy of the aim, the pull of the trigger. Everything. I took it to a gun shop here in town and found out that it was probably customized by a place in Arkansas that does special orders for police SWAT teams, the FBI, and some of the elite forces of the military. Like the Navy SEALs, for instance.''

"The Navy SEALs—'' Grace broke off, gasping. She stared at Ethan in open shock. "My God. What are you saying?''

He stopped pacing and turned to watch her for a long moment before moving toward the bed. Grace had to fight the urge to retreat.

He placed his hands on the bed and leaned toward her, his eyes those of a stranger. "I'm saying that I don't know who I am. I don't know how to explain everything that's happened to me, the dreams I have, the shoes that don't fit, the gun that was custom-made for me. Even the connection you and I seem to have.''

He paused, his gaze intensifying on her until Grace's breath became suspended somewhere in her throat. "What I'm saying is that for all I know, I could be the man you're looking for. I could be Trevor Reardon.''

Chapter Twelve

Grace put a hand to her mouth to hold back the scream that tore at her throat. She stared at the space where Ethan had stood only moments before, and nausea rose in her stomach like a tidal wave.

He wasn't Trevor Reardon. She knew it couldn't be true, and yet the moment Ethan had said the words, the doubts had begun to mount inside her. She hadn't been able to hold back her horrified gasp, and when Ethan had seen her face, he'd turned and strode from the room, slamming the door behind him.

The sound still echoed in the silent room. His words still rang in her ears. Grace shook her head, trying to dispel the almost hypnotic effect his words had had on her. She couldn't move, couldn't think, couldn't reason.

Weakly she reached for her purse on the nightstand. Taking out her cell phone, she dialed Myra's number. The throaty voice answered on the second ring.

Without preamble, Grace said, "Did you hear back from the fingerprints you sent to the lab?"

If Myra had been sleeping, she gave no indication of it. She sounded wide awake and fully alert. "The ones we lifted from Dr. Hunter's clinic?" Grace heard

Myra's lighter click open as she lit up a cigarette. "Strange that you should be calling about that."

Grace was instantly alarmed. "Why?"

Myra hesitated. "Actually, we lifted several sets of prints from Dr. Hunter's office, some from around the desk area that we were pretty certain were his. But just as a control, we also took some from the water glass in his hospital room." She paused to take a long drag on her cigarette. Grace wanted to scream in frustration. "When we ran all the prints through the computer, we found that the ones from the glass were flagged."

Grace sat on the edge of the bed, frowning. "Flagged? By whom?"

"I don't know yet."

"Wait a minute," Grace said. "Are you saying the prints from the glass didn't match any of the prints in Dr. Hunter's office?"

"No, they did. Only, the prints that were a match didn't belong to Dr. Hunter."

Grace gripped the phone until her knuckles hurt. "Myra, are you saying the man in this house with me isn't Ethan Hunter?"

There was another long pause. Then Myra said slowly, "It's possible."

Grace's breath rushed from her lungs in a long, painful swish. "Just when the hell were you going to tell me?"

"As soon as I had all the facts. Listen, Grace, I just got this information myself a little while ago. I didn't know what to make of it. I've been trying to find out what I could from the Information Division, but they haven't been exactly forthcoming. It's all hush-hush. I don't understand what it all means yet, but Connelly said the lab is suddenly crawling with agents."

"FBI?"

"He doesn't think so."

"Then who?"

"We don't know, but if that man isn't Ethan Hunter, then someone else is looking for him. And not only that, they want to make damned sure they know when and if someone else finds him. That's why the prints were flagged, and now Connelly is catching hell."

"What has he told them?"

"Nothing yet, and he won't until he finds out just exactly who and what we're up against." Myra paused again. "It may be time to pull you out, Grace."

Grace's heart was thumping so hard against her chest she thought her ribcage might explode. But she had never been one to walk away from an assignment until it was finished. And this one was far from over.

She drew a long breath, trying to calm her racing pulse. "If we pull out now, the whole operation craters. We may never find Reardon. I don't want to run that risk. Until we find out what's going on, I think I should stay put."

"This could get very sticky," Myra warned.

"I'm aware of that."

After a moment, Myra said, "Maybe you're right. Whoever he is, he had us fooled. He may be able to fool Trevor Reardon as well."

Grace's mind was a whirlwind of chaotic thoughts. After hanging up the phone, she paced the room nervously. Never had she been so unsure of a situation before, so out of control of an operation as she was at that moment.

Who was he? her mind screamed. Who the hell was he?

Spinning toward the nightstand, Grace grabbed her

gun and gripped it in one hand while crossing the floor to lock her bedroom door. And all the while she kept telling herself that what she was thinking, what Ethan had suggested was crazy. He couldn't be Trevor Reardon. She would have known, for God's sake. He couldn't have fooled her again. Not so completely.

Her legs shaking with nerves, Grace sat down in a chair facing the bedroom door. She propped her feet on the edge of the bed and put the gun in her lap. There would be no sleep for her tonight, but just to be on the safe side, she wouldn't lie down. She would remain in this chair, awake and vigilant, until morning came and with it, hopefully answers.

YOU'RE SO BEAUTIFUL. Do you have an idea how special you are to me, Grace?

Trevor Reardon's voice awakened Grace with a start. She gasped and grabbed her gun, aiming at first one spot in the room and then the next.

It took her a long, terrified moment to realize she was alone in the room and she'd been dreaming.

Reardon's voice, whispering in her ear, came back to her and a shiver of dread tore up Grace's spine. The dream had seemed so real. She had heard his voice so clearly, that indefinable quality that had haunted her for years.

Grace thought she'd only dozed off for a few seconds, but when she glanced at the clock on the bedside table, she realized she'd been asleep for almost an hour. It was nearly three o'clock in the morning and the moon was up. The sterling light danced along the fringes of the room, deepening the shadows in the corners.

The moon glow was what alerted Grace first. Earlier,

she'd turned on the lamp on the nightstand, but now it was off. And the faintest scent of men's cologne lingered in the air.

Grace's heart boomeranged against her chest. Ethan hadn't been wearing cologne earlier. He'd come straight to her room from the shower, his hair still damp and smelling of shampoo, his skin scented only with soap.

But the smell of cologne on the air was unmistakable.

Slowly, Grace got up from the chair, her weapon drawn. The first thing she did was search the bathroom, then she crossed the bedroom to the door. It was still locked, and for a moment, she told herself she was imagining things.

But that whisper came back to her. *You're so beautiful. Do you have any idea how special you are to me, Grace?*

And she knew without a doubt it had been no dream. Reardon—or someone—had been in this room with her. He'd managed to pick the lock on her bedroom door, but that was no surprise. The flimsy bolt wouldn't keep out a determined ten-year-old, let alone a criminal mastermind.

No, the surprising part was how easily he'd been able to slip through the surveillance surrounding the house, and then disable the alarm without detection. Unless, of course, he'd been in the house all along.

Grace closed her eyes, terror stealing over her. She gripped the pistol, forcing herself to open the bedroom door and move out into the hallway. But with every step she took, she heard Ethan's warning. *I'm saying that I don't know who I am, Grace. I don't know how to explain everything that's happened to me, the dreams I have, the shoes that don't fit, the gun that was custom-made for me. Even the connection you and I seem to have.*

Grace was on the stairs now, moving stealthily downward. The living room below was silent. Eerie. The shadows ghostly in the moonlight.

She came to the bottom of the stairs and moved into the living room.

What I'm saying is that for all I know, I could be the man you're looking for.

Slowly, Grace crossed the living room toward the study. A thin line of light glowed at the bottom of the closed door. Someone was inside.

I could be Trevor Reardon.

Grace paused outside the door, catching her breath and steeling her nerves. Then she reached out and swung the door inward.

Ethan sat behind the desk, his face dimly illuminated by a lamp that had been angled away from him. He looked up when Grace entered, seemingly unconcerned by the gun she had pointed at him, and smiled. A smile that was as charming as it was inherently evil.

Chapter Thirteen

The man seated behind the desk was Ethan, and he wasn't.

Grace couldn't quite believe her eyes. She blinked once, then again, but the face before her didn't change.

She saw almost immediately that the faces weren't identical, but there was a very strong resemblance. This man, Dr. Hunter she presumed, was a little smoother around the edges. Polished to a high gloss of sophistication, while the Ethan she knew was tougher, more dangerous looking.

However, as Dr. Hunter rose and came around the desk to stand in front of her, Grace thought her initial assessment of him might have been wrong. The glint of greed and deadly determination in his eyes was unmistakable.

"Where's Ethan?" She kept the gun leveled on him.

Dr. Hunter cocked a dark brow, very reminiscent of the man she knew as Ethan. "You mean my look-alike? Don't worry, he's safe. For the time being, at least."

Grace wondered what that meant. Her hand trembled slightly on the gun, but she used all of her resolve to steady it. "Where is he?" Her tone hardened with threat. "I want to see him."

"You will," Dr. Hunter said. "But I've a few things here I have to take care of first."

"I don't think you're in any position to bargain," Grace said coldly. "In case you hadn't noticed, I'm the one with the gun here."

"Oh, I couldn't help but notice," Hunter said smoothly. Then his voice hardened. "But in case you hadn't noticed, we aren't exactly alone."

And with that, a man stepped through the door behind Grace and put a gun barrel to her head. "Drop the gun, *por favor,*" he said with a heavy Spanish accent.

When Grace hesitated, Dr. Hunter said, "Better do as he says. For all his gentle appearance, Javier can be quite vicious. Besides which, you can't possibly take us both out."

He was right about that. When Grace lowered her weapon, the man behind her reached down and took it from her hand. Then he tossed it to Dr. Hunter.

The man called Javier walked slowly around Grace, still keeping the weapon drawn on her. When he was in front of her, she stared at him, recognizing the dark hair, the coal eyes, the thin, black mustache. He was the man she'd seen in the corridor outside the ballroom of the Huntington Hotel, the man she had pursued into the laundry room, and possibly the man who had murdered Special Agent Huddleston.

"You already know who I am," Dr. Hunter was saying "This is a colleague of mine, Dr. Javier Salizar. He runs the clinic in Mexico when I'm not around. It's been a mutually advantageous arrangement over the years, but now that I'm bowing out, he'll be free to use the clinic to continue the small but very powerful drug cartel he's building.''

Salizar made an abrupt movement with his gun, one that had Grace's heart pounding in alarm.

Dr. Hunter put up a hand, as if to restrain his colleague. He said something in rapid Spanish, then to Grace he said, ''But I still don't know your name.''

She saw no reason not to tell him. ''Grace Donovan.''

''FBI, I presume?''

She shrugged.

''Well, at least you're not denying it,'' he said. ''Not that it matters. Now that you've seen me, I'm sure you realize I can't let you go.''

''Is that why you killed Huddleston?'' When Hunter glanced at her blankly, she said, ''The agent at the Huntington Hotel.''

''Ah.'' Hunter steepled his fingers beneath his chin. ''He saw me at the hotel while he was shadowing Pilar and Bob. I couldn't let him go after that.''

Grace glanced at the gun in Salizar's hand, then at Dr. Hunter, assessing her situation. Unfortunately, she didn't see a way out. Not yet at least. ''How did you get in here?''

''Past your surveillance, you mean? It was pathetically easy. We were back here before you arrived from the Huntington.''

''But Ethan told me he changed the alarm code.''

''So he did, but I almost always have a backup plan. Once when I came back from Mexico, my loving wife had changed the code so that I couldn't get into my own house. After that, I had the security company program in an override code that only I knew. Pilar never pulled that stunt again.''

The smile vanished from his face, leaving in its place a cruel sneer that made Grace shiver. If she had underestimated Dr. Hunter's capabilities before, she would not do so now.

"Why did you give him your face?" she asked suddenly.

The charming smile was back in place. He shrugged nonchalantly. "Because I knew Reardon would come after me. And if not him, then some other criminal whose face I've changed. They're all extremely grateful at first, but then they get to thinking. Paranoia sets in. Their plastic surgeon is the only one who can identify them. Sooner or later, one of them was bound to come after me."

Grace frowned. "So you created yourself a double? How did you think you could pull that off? Eventually someone would catch on."

"Not if the double was dead," Dr. Hunter said with another shrug. "I had it all planned out very carefully. Or so I thought," he added ironically. "I brought him back to Houston, dumped him in my clinic, and then one of Dr. Salizar's American associates was to shoot him in the face before he came to and make the whole thing look like robbery. Only, your friend decided to wake up before he was supposed to, and he managed to save himself. Imagine my surprise when I found out what had happened, that my look-alike was still alive and poking around in my life, digging up secrets I didn't want exposed."

"An autopsy would have revealed he wasn't you," Grace said. "You couldn't change blood types, fingerprints, DNA."

"There was no reason to," Dr. Hunter said almost impatiently. "With both Amy and him dead in the clinic, there would have been no reason to suspect he wasn't me. Especially since I'd made sure my passport and ID were on him, along with my wedding ring. There would have been no need for anything other than the most rudimentary autopsy, and I'd taken care of the blood type by changing my medical records at the hospital before I went out of the country. I thought of everything.''

Not everything, Grace thought. She wondered if she should tell him about the fingerprints, about the fact that the FBI were on to him. But if cornered, he might become even more desperate, and Grace wasn't willing to admit yet that she couldn't somehow find a way out of this.

''Who is he?'' she tried to ask without emotion. ''Where did you find him?''

Dr. Hunter smiled. ''That's the beauty of it. He's no one anybody would ever come looking for, except maybe for the police. He was affiliated with one of Dr. Salizar's rival drug cartels, and the Mexican authorities shot him while he was trying to escape capture.''

Affiliated with a drug cartel? A sour taste rose to Grace's mouth. *He's no one anybody would come looking for, except maybe the police.*

Not Trevor Reardon, she thought weakly, but someone perhaps just as dark.

''Apparently, he fell off a cliff, and some of the locals found him and brought him to me,'' Dr. Hunter said. ''I'll spare you the details, but suffice to say, his face was badly damaged, and he had a severe head trauma which resulted in acute amnesia. When he woke up, he didn't remember who he was or how he'd gotten to the clinic. He remained heavily sedated at the clinic while I came back here. He couldn't remember his past before he arrived at the clinic, and the drugs ensured he wouldn't remember his time there. We were spared a lot of questions that way. I even brought his gun back here with me so there would be no way to identify him. Once his wounds had healed sufficiently, I went back to Mexico and began the reconstruction on his face. He didn't remember anything about his former life, so I gave him a new one."

She lifted her chin, staring Hunter straight in the eyes. "I'm a federal agent," she said. "This house in under surveillance. The minute you fire one of those guns, the place will be crawling with FBI."

"You mean the three men watching the house? Javier's American *amigo* has taken care of them for us."

The sick feeling inside Grace deepened. Three more agents dead? God—

Dr. Hunter turned to Salizar and spoke rapidly in Spanish, something about the American Salizar had apparently hired for the job. As best Grace could tell, there'd been a last minute change in plans, and in spite of Hunter's cool demeanor, he was worried about the new man.

When Hunter turned back to Grace, she said, "What are you going to do with me?"

He shrugged. "Oh, I have plans for you. Lofty plans, you might say."

Dr. Salizar had moved behind her, and now Grace saw Dr. Hunter nod to him over her shoulder. She whirled, automatically putting up a hand to defend herself, but she was too late. The butt of the gun caught her square in the back of the head.

With a blinding flash of pain, Grace pitched face forward to the floor.

WHEN SHE AWAKENED, the pain was a dull roar in her head. She lay facedown in what she first thought must be a van or a truck, but the rumble of engines below her and the sway and dip as they hit air pockets told her they were airborne.

She struggled to rise, but her head swam sickeningly, and when she tried to move, she realized her hands were bound behind her. With an effort, she rolled to her side, then managed to sit up, gazing around.

Ethan was directly in front of her, leaning against the wall of the plane, his hands behind him and his eyes closed. One side of his face was covered in blood, and Grace's heart lurched in terror. For one heart-stopping moment, she was positive he was dead. He was so still and his face was deathly pale.

But then very slowly he opened his eyes and focused on her. A look of intense relief flooded over his features, and Grace realized he must have been conscious for some time now, and wondering the same thing about her.

"Are you all right?" he whispered, throwing a glance toward the front of the plane.

Grace nodded, unsure of her voice. "Are you?"

"I will be, as soon as I get these ropes loose."

His brow wrinkled in concentration as he strained at the bindings. Grace glanced around, assessing their situation. They were in the rear of the plane. Luggage and crates of supplies were stacked near the back, and directly opposite, a door opened to the front. Grace could see two or three rows of seat backs, and beyond that, a curtain that closed off the cockpit.

The cargo door was on the wall nearest her, but without parachutes, the exit wouldn't do them much good.

She glanced back at Ethan. "What happened?" she whispered.

"They were waiting for me when I came back downstairs. They were in the house when we got back from the hotel."

"Yes, I know. The agents watching the house are dead."

Ethan's eyes flickered briefly as he struggled with the ropes.

"Where are they taking us?" Grace asked, working at her own bindings. Her wrists grew raw from the effort.

"I heard them mention Mexico. Hunter still thinks he can pull this off."

Grace glanced up. "You've seen him then?"

Ethan's gaze met hers, and something dark flashed in his eyes. "I've seen him."

Grace wondered what he was thinking, what it must have felt like to come face to face with his reflection. She tried to temper the rush of emotion she felt for him by reminding herself of what Hunter had told her—that the man she knew as Ethan had been involved with a drug cartel in Mexico.

But looking at him now, Grace couldn't bring herself to believe it. Didn't want to believe it. If he never got his memory back, would that side of him disappear forever?

Could he live with that? And could she?

Maybe it was all a moot point anyway if they couldn't find a way out of their current predicament.

As if reading her mind, Ethan said, "He still thinks he can get rid of me and have everyone believe he's dead."

"It's been him all along," Grace said. "Not Reardon. Hunter hired someone to kill both you and Amy so that everyone would think he was dead.''

"Not a bad plan," Ethan said dryly.

"Except for the fact that the FBI knows you and he are not one and the same man.''

Ethan's movements ceased. He looked up at her. "What?"

"We lifted some prints from the water glass in your hospital room and ran them through the national database. My superior knows that you're not Dr. Hunter.''

"Who am I?" A look Grace couldn't identify crossed over his features. Fear. Dread. Hope. Uncertainty.

What could she tell him that would alleviate his worry? "You aren't Trevor Reardon," she said.

"Then who am I?"

"I...don't know yet."

His gaze on her hardened. "How long have you known this? From the first?"

Grace shook her head. "No. No. I just found out tonight. I didn't have a chance to tell you—"

Before she could finish, a shadowed blackened the doorway to the front of the plane, and Grace looked up to find Dr. Hunter staring down at her. It was still so uncanny to see how much he looked like Ethan.

Grace glanced at Ethan. His gaze was riveted to Dr. Hunter. She couldn't imagine what this must be like for him. For the first time that night, she wondered what he'd looked like before the surgery.

"You're both awake, I see." Dr. Hunter moved into the cargo area, and Dr. Salizar followed him. Salizar carried a gun in his hand, and another gun—Grace's—was stuck in the front waistband of his khaki trousers.

Hunter walked over to one of the crates, opened it,

and extracted three parachutes. He handed one of the chutes to Salizar, then buckled himself into the other.

"Go tell your amigo it's time to set the automatic pilot," he told Salizar. "I hope to God you're right about him, Javier. I hope he can be trusted."

Salizar handed Hunter one of the guns. "Don't worry. Julio vouched for him."

"That makes me feel so much better," Hunter muttered.

A fine dread slipped over Grace as she realized his intent. He, Salizar, and the pilot would parachute from the plane, leaving Ethan and Grace tied up inside.

She glanced at Ethan, but his gaze was still on Hunter. "Who am I?" he asked suddenly.

Hunter arched a brow at Grace. "You didn't tell him?"

Grace felt Ethan's gaze on her and she turned to him quickly. "He didn't tell me who you are. I swear it."

Hunter laughed. "I didn't give you a name, but I did give you a few details. But don't worry," he said to Ethan. "You two will have an hour, maybe two before the fuel runs out. Or before you crash into a mountain."

Grace said almost desperately, "You'll never get away with this. The FBI knows Ethan isn't you. They have his fingerprints."

That stopped Hunter for a moment. He stood gazing down at Grace, a frown playing between his brows. "Well, that is unfortunate, but it can't be helped. I guess instead of playing dead, I'll just have to disappear somewhere and live out the rest of my life on my Swiss and Cayman Island bank accounts. Which is exactly what I intended to do anyway."

"But now you'll be a hunted man," Grace said.

"You're a murderer. The FBI will track you to the ends of the earth, not to mention Trevor Reardon."

A man came through the door behind Hunter. He wore a red baseball cap pulled down low over his features. In one hand, he carried a parachute; in the other, one of Salizar's guns.

Hunter said over his shoulder, "Where's Javier?"

"He'll be along in a minute." The man kept his head bowed, as if studying the parachute in his hand.

"Is everything all set in the cockpit?" Hunter asked him.

The man nodded, then walked over to the cargo door, threw back the catch, and slid the door open.

A rush of wind streamed inside, the fury catching Grace off guard. For a moment, she was afraid the force might pull her through the opening. She worked even harder at the ropes around her wrist. When she glanced at Ethan, she could tell he was doing the same thing. His gaze on her seemed to say, "Hang in there. We'll get out of this somehow."

Grace desperately wanted to believe him, but even if they got free of the ropes, Hunter, Salizar, and the pilot were all armed.

Hunter finished buckling his parachute and turned back to Grace. "You can stop worrying about Reardon," he shouted over the roar of wind through the opening. "His cleverness has been greatly overrated. I've managed to stay one step ahead of him so far, and where I'm going now, he'll never find me."

"Is that so?" The man wearing the red cap looked up, and for a moment, Grace stared at him in puzzlement. Then, as if in slow motion, he lifted his hand and removed the cap from his head, revealing a receding hairline.

Dr. Hunter swung around, reaching for his weapon. But Danny Medford had a gun leveled at Hunter's chest, and Grace saw horror and recognition dawn on the doctor's face.

"Reardon!"

It didn't register with Grace what Medford's sudden appearance meant at first, but then, as the realization hit her, she turned to stare at him, terror spiraling through.

"You're—" She couldn't even say his name. Before she could hardly catch her breath, he fired the gun, and a stunned look crossed over Dr. Hunter's features. Then he slumped to the floor.

Reardon bent down and with a knife, cut away the straps of Hunter's parachute. Then he tossed the blade aside, and rolled the body out the open cargo door.

Grace's heart pounded inside her. She turned to stare at Ethan. She could tell from his expression he was as shocked as she was. And he was still working to free himself from his ropes.

Reardon walked over to Grace and stood grinning down at her. For the first time, Grace saw behind his new face and the contacts he wore, to the evil that couldn't be masked. "What's the matter, Grace? Don't you recognize me?"

Fourteen years ago, he had been the handsomest man Grace had ever seen. Now his features were almost plain, his good looks sacrificed for his freedom.

He knelt, caressing her face with the barrel of his gun—her gun, she recognized. Obviously, he'd killed Dr. Salizar and taken the gun from him.

Reardon put his hand around Grace's neck, and her skin crawled at his touch. Her stomach rolled sickeningly. When she would have jerked away, he said,

"You're so beautiful. Do you have any idea how special you are to me?"

Grace felt the bile rising in her throat. On the other side of the plane, she could see Ethan openly struggling at his ropes. Reardon noticed him, too, and nodded in Ethan's direction. "I see the clone wants to come to your rescue."

Ethan looked up, his gaze meeting Reardon's. The look on Ethan's face chilled Grace to the bone. He was a match for Reardon. She had no doubt of it.

Reardon must have sensed it, too, for he stood abruptly and disappeared through the door to the front of the plane. When he came back moments later, he had Salizar's chute. He tossed it out the door. Grace saw the wind whip it away in a blur.

The only parachute left on board was Reardon's. He came back to stand over Grace, and for a moment, she thought the end had come. He was going to finish her off.

Ethan said, "You touch her, and I'll kill you."

Reardon cocked his head, staring at Ethan. "Do you know who I am?"

Ethan almost smiled. "Yes. And that's going to make killing you all the more pleasurable."

A look that might have been admiration flashed in Reardon's eyes. Or was it fear?

Then he laughed, a sound that took Grace straight back to that night fourteen years ago. She closed her eyes as the horror swept over her.

"I admire your nerve, my friend, but you are hardly in any position to make threats." He turned to Grace. "And you. Imagine my surprise when I followed Hunter to the clinic that night and saw you there. After all these years, we finally meet again, Grace. I believe it's destiny, don't you?''

When Grace didn't answer, he said, "You've made everything very convenient for me. I can take care of you and Dr. Hunter in one fell swoop, and you—" He turned back to Ethan. "You've seen my new face, so I'm afraid it's *adiós* for you as well. The only thing left for me to do," he said, walking over to the open door and preparing to strap on his parachute, "is to look up my old friend, Myra."

Grace strained at her ropes. She couldn't let Reardon get away. She couldn't let him get to Myra. As she struggled furiously with the bindings, something caught her eye. A flash of metal. The knife Reardon had tossed aside.

"Oh, and one last thing," he said, turning back to Grace. "That last night you and I spent together. I called your father when you'd gone into the bathroom. You didn't know that, did you? The last thing on his mind before he died was the knowledge that his precious daughter was with me. I wanted you to know that before you die."

Fury swept over Grace in a blinding flash. She lunged at Reardon, but before she could reach him, before he even had time to sense her intention, Ethan was on him. Somehow he'd gotten loose from his ropes, and now the force of his attack almost sent both him and Reardon plunging out the open door. Reardon dropped the parachute, and Grace saw it slip over the side of the door.

Both men fell to the floor of the plane, the gun in Reardon's hand whipping upward before Ethan could grab his wrist. Then he slammed Reardon's hand against the floor of the plane, and the gun went flying.

The fight was ugly. The men were evenly matched, one as deadly and cold-blooded as the other.

Grace scooted sideways, turning so she could get one hand around the knife. Twisting it awkwardly, she began to saw at the ropes around her wrist.

Her heart almost stopping, Grace saw Reardon roll toward the open doorway, pulling Ethan with him. With a vicious kick, Reardon sent Ethan half over the edge. Ethan clung to the metal frame around the opening, but the wind force almost ripped him away. Grace could see the strain on his face, the sheer force of his willpower as he began to pull himself inside.

Reardon stood poised in the open doorway, clinging to an overhead support to brace himself against the rush of wind as he stared down at Ethan.

Desperately, Grace hacked at the ropes around her wrist, felt the sting of pain as the blade found skin. Then she was free. In one fluid movement, she rolled on the floor and grabbed the gun just as Reardon lifted his foot to kick Ethan loose from the door.

Grace screamed Reardon's name over the rush of wind and when he turned to her, she saw his eyes widen in surprise at the gun in her hand. Without hesitation, Grace pulled the trigger. The force of the bullet, combined with the wind velocity, knocked Reardon from the plane. Grace heard him scream and saw the scarlet bloom on his chest before he disappeared into the darkness.

In a flash, she was on her knees in front of the doorway. She grabbed Ethan's arms and helped pull him inside. They lay panting on the floor of the plane for a long moment before Grace scrambled back to the opening, peering out into the darkness.

"He's dead, Grace. You got him," Ethan said.

Grace turned back, her gaze uncertain. "I hope you're right. God, I hope you're right."

They stared at each other, letting the adrenaline rush carry the emotions through their bloodstream. Then Grace said, "I don't suppose you knew how to fly a plane before your amnesia?"

Ethan's gaze darkened for a moment, and then he said, almost grimly, "I think I might have."

Chapter Fourteen

They were on the ground at an airfield just across the border from Brownsville, Texas. Grace was in the police magistrate's office, talking with Myra on the telephone and filling her in on all the details.

Myra listened, and then when Grace was finished, said, "After all these years, you finally got him. How does it feel?"

Grace hadn't had time to deal with her emotions. She supposed what she felt most strongly at that moment was uncertainty, about her future and about Ethan's. She said almost urgently, "What's happening on your end? Have you found out anything else about the fingerprints?"

A long hesitation, then Myra said, "Turns out, the agency who flagged his prints is the DEA, Grace. Evidently they've been looking for him for a long time, and now they're demanding that we turn him over to them."

Grace sucked in a long breath. "Are you sure? There could have been a mistake. A computer glitch."

"There's no mistake. You've got to bring him in, Grace. You don't have a choice."

ETHAN COULD TELL from the look on Grace's face that the call hadn't gone well. "You talked to your superior?"

She nodded. She started to say something else, then turned to stare across the street at a seedy-looking bar that blasted tejano music.

"Let's take a walk," she suggested. "It's a little noisy around here."

They strolled along the cobblestone sidewalk until they reached the edge of town. The night seemed darker over the desert, with only a few stars and the moon to soften the gloom. In a few hours, it would be dawn, but right now, daylight still seemed a long way off.

Without looking at her, Ethan said, "I'm going back to the jungle, Grace. Back to that clinic. I have to find out who I am. I have to know...what I've done."

"Ethan—"

He took her arms, turning her to face him. He stared down into her eyes, feeling the connection with her as he had never felt it before. Maybe because he was about to sever it.

"That call you just made. What you found out wasn't good, was it?"

He saw the denial flicker over her features, then she closed her eyes briefly. "It doesn't matter."

"Yes, it does." His grip tightened on her arms. "You're a cop, Grace. An FBI agent sworn to uphold the law. How can you say who I am and what I've done doesn't matter?"

She gazed up at him. "Going back to the jungle may be the most dangerous place for you. If you come back with me—"

"You'll see that they go easy on me?" He shook

his head. "I'm not above the law, Grace. If I've done something wrong, something...bad, then I'll take my punishment for it. But not until I find out the truth for myself. Not until I know the whole story. Can you understand that?"

What he was asking of her went against everything she stood for, everything she believed in. A wave of guilt rolled over Ethan for what he was about to do, but there was no other way.

He took a step back from her, and he saw her bewilderment in the moonlight. Then her disbelief.

He took another step away from her, backing into the desert as he leveled the gun on her.

"It's the only way, Grace. I can't ask you to give up everything for me. I won't. So don't try to follow me." It was more of a plea than a warning, but for one split second, he sensed her resistance.

"This isn't goodbye," he promised.

"Then why do I feel like it is?" she said, before turning and walking away.

GRACE SAT IN the cubicle Myra had confiscated at the Houston office and tried to ignore the tension that fairly sizzled in the room. Two huge men wearing black suits and identical scowls stood on either side of Grace while Myra sat across a metal desk from her. When Grace had first entered the office, less than twenty-four hours after her flight back from the border, Myra had introduced the two men as her counterparts at the DEA. Which meant they had considerable clout.

Myra folded her arms on the top of the desk and said, "Please tell Agents Mackelroy and Delaney what you told me, Grace."

Grace glanced up at first one man, and then the other. She shrugged. "He got away."

Mackelroy, the larger of the two men, came around to perch on the edge of Myra's desk. "How?"

"He pulled a gun on me."

She could see the disbelief in the man's eyes before he flashed a glance at his partner. Mackelroy said, "Tell us exactly what happened."

Grace complied, leaving out only the part she deemed too personal for them to hear. Some of what had gone down between her and Ethan was none of their damned business.

Mackelroy leaned toward Grace, his gaze intense. "Do you have any idea where he is now? It's imperative that we find him."

Grace met his gaze. "Why do you want him so badly? Who is he?"

The two men exchanged another glance. Then Mackelroy said almost urgently, "His name is Tony Stark. He's one of our agents. For the last two years, he's been under deep cover, infiltrating one of the drug cartels down in Mexico."

For a moment, Grace thought she hadn't heard him correctly. She stared at him, stunned. Then she said slowly, "He's a DEA agent?"

Mackelroy nodded. "The last we heard, he'd been arrested by some local authorities who were working for a rival cartel. Somehow he managed to escape, and then he just disappeared. We assumed he was dead, but then his fingerprints turned up in the computer. The rest you know."

Grace felt as if she had just been sucker punched. She couldn't breathe, much less talk.

Myra said throatily, "Of course, we'd like to cooperate as much as we can, but Grace has told you everything. Stark is down in Mexico somewhere, wandering around without a memory. If he were one of my agents, I wouldn't waste time in getting down there to find him.''

BY THE END of the week, Grace was back home in Washington. She'd filed the last of her reports and attended one final debriefing before leaving the J. Edgar Hoover Building in a downpour.

She stood at the window of her apartment, and stared out at the city. It was Friday, past eight o'clock, and the city was coming alive. The streets were still clogged with government workers and officials wending their way southward, to the suburbs in Maryland and Virginia. The ones who lived in the city were finding little pockets of shelter in the hundreds of bars and bistros scattered throughout Washington.

The rain had stopped a little while ago, and a breeze drifted in from the Potomac River. The heat of the day gave way to a crisp coolness of evening, and the sky deepened to violet.

Grace had never felt more at loose ends after wrapping up a case, because this had been no ordinary case. Trevor Reardon was dead, and for the first time in fourteen years, she felt the weight of her guilt begin to ease. She knew she could let go of the past now, say goodbye to a family she would never stop missing.

But in some strange way, the emptiness inside her had deepened. The lonely years of her life stretched before her, and Grace suddenly realized how much she'd given up to her dedication. A home. A family. A man she could love.

A future that made her want to get up in the mornings.

Ethan had done this to her, Grace thought without bitterness. Ethan had made her realize what she was missing, what her sacrifices had cost her. He had reminded her that she had once been capable of love. Might still be.

She closed her eyes briefly, resting her forehead against the cool glass. She wondered where he was now, if he was safe, if he had been found by the DEA and told who he was. What he was.

She had known all along there was goodness in him.

Grace turned when the doorbell sounded and reluctantly left her place at the window to answer it, figuring it was Myra trying to talk her out of the resignation Grace had tendered after her last debriefing. But it was time for a change. Time to try her hand at being a lawyer, which was what she'd always wanted to be.

She pulled back the door. "I'm not changing my mind, Myra—"

Ethan stood on the other side, dressed in jeans and a dark cotton shirt, a raincoat slung over his shoulder. His dark hair glistened with moisture as he gazed down at her uncertainly.

"I wasn't sure this was the right place," he finally said.

Grace stepped back to let him enter. "How did you find me?"

"Some of my friends at the DEA office in Houston helped track you down."

Grace's heart quickened. "Then you know?"

"A couple of agents were waiting for me at Hunter's clinic down in Mexico. I guess they somehow figured out I'd be going there to find some answers." He gave Grace a pointed look, and she quickly turned away.

"It would seem a logical place to start searching for you," she said, leading him into the living room. She glanced around at the dismal atmosphere of her home. Come Monday morning, she was going to start redecorating, Grace decided. A new career, a new apartment, a whole new life.

Where would Ethan fit into her plans? she wondered. Or would he want to?

She motioned toward the sofa, but they both remained standing. "I've been wondering about you, you know. Where you were. How you were doing. There're a lot of things we've left unsaid, Ethan."

He smiled, and Grace caught her breath. He looked different all of a sudden. Like a new man. "My name is Tony."

She smiled, too, her heart pounding inside her. "I know, but that'll take some getting used to."

He watched her move toward the window. She stood with her back to the glow of city lights, and the way she looked almost took his breath away.

He walked over to stand beside her, and they both turned to stare out at the glistening night. "I don't have my memory back," he finally said. "Not all of it, but bits and pieces are starting to come back. And I've been told quite a lot." He turned to her. "I've seen pictures of myself, the way I looked before. Unless I agree to more surgery, I guess I'm stuck with this face."

"It's a nice face," Grace said softly.

"You don't think of...*him* when you look at me? You don't feel revulsion?"

She reached up and touched his cheek very briefly

with her fingertips. "I see you. No one else. It doesn't matter what you look like. Appearances are only skin deep. It's who you are that counts."

He gazed down at her, resisting the urge to touch the fiery strands of her hair, to let the softness sift through his fingers.

She turned back to the window, but he could see that she was watching his reflection. After a moment, she said, "It must seem so strange, finding out about yourself like that. You must have had a million questions."

His gaze met hers in the window. "There was one question in particular I was anxious to find the answer to."

She faced him. Her eyes were very clear and very blue. He thought she had never looked more beautiful. "What question was that?"

He did touch her then, lifting his hand to smooth back her hair, letting his fingers slip through the silkiness. He saw her eyes close briefly. "Can't you guess?"

She took a breath. "Are you married?"

He grinned. "That's the one."

"And?" she asked impatiently, folding her arms across her breasts. She put up a good front, but Tony was gratified to see the flash of uncertainty in her eyes.

"I'm not married," he said softly. "Never have been."

"And never will be?" she challenged, the doubt in her eyes changing to a teasing glint.

"I wouldn't say that." He raised his other hand and threaded his fingers through her hair, then kissed her. Her lips quivered beneath his, and Tony thought in wonder what an incredible woman she was. A woman who could face a cold-blooded killer without showing fear, but one who trembled at his kiss.

He pulled back, staring into her eyes. "The connection is still there, Grace. Do you feel it?"

"Yes." She smiled. "Oh, yes."

"The question now is, what are we going to do about it?"

She looked up at him slyly. "You could kiss me again." After he complied, she said, "We have some unfinished business, you and I."

Her boldness thrilled him. "We've got all night. There's nowhere in the world I have to be."

She slipped her arms around his neck. "As a matter of fact, I find myself in the same situation. I'm not an FBI agent anymore," she told him. "I resigned today."

He lifted his brows at that, but instead of asking her why, he said, "I'm not a DEA agent anymore, either. I wouldn't be much good in the field without a memory."

Grace sighed deeply, but it wasn't an unhappy sound. More one of relief. "So what are we going to do?"

He wrapped his arms around her, pulling her close. "I don't know, but we have the rest of our lives to figure it out. I do know one thing. I want to get to know you, Grace. I want to know everything about you. The last few days don't seem real somehow. I want to spend time with you without looking over my shoulder. Without wondering if this moment will be our last."

"Wow," Grace breathed. "You want all that? And here I thought we were just going to spend the night together."

"That's a start," he said seriously. "Believe me, that'll be one hell of a start."

If you enjoyed what you just read,
then we've got an offer you can't resist!

Take 2 bestselling love stories FREE!

Plus get a FREE surprise gift!

MURDER AT THE MOVIES

CHARLENE WEIR
GEORGE BAXT
MAXINE O'CALLAGHAN

MURDER TAKE TWO
by Charlene Weir

Hollywood comes to Hampstead, Kansas, with the filming of a
new picture starring sexy actress Laura Edwards. But murder
steals the scene when a stunt double is impaled on a pitchfork.

THE HUMPHREY BOGART MURDER CASE
by George Baxt

Hollywood in its heyday is brought to life in this witty caper
featuring a surprise sleuth—Humphrey Bogart. While filming
The Maltese Falcon, he searches for a real-life treasure, dodging
a killer on a murder trail through Hollywood.

SOMEWHERE SOUTH OF MELROSE
by Maxine O'Callaghan

P.I. Delilah West is hired to search for an old high school
classmate. The path takes her through the underbelly of broken
dreams and into the caprices of fate, where secrets are born and
sometimes kept....

Available March 1999 at your favorite retail outlet.

Look us up on-line at: http://www.worldwidemystery.com   WMOM305

COMING NEXT MONTH

#513 THE STRANGER SHE KNEW by Gayle Wilson
Men of Mystery

Ex-CIA agent Jordan Cross was given a new face and a new life.
What he didn't know was that his new identity belonged to a man
with dangerous enemies—and now he's put an innocent woman and
her children in jeopardy.

#514 THE BODYGUARD by Sheryl Lynn
Elk River, Colorado

J. T. McKennon was everything a man was supposed to be. Loyal,
strong, responsible and determined—not to mention the way he could
kiss. And as a bodyguard he was the ultimate protector. But as far as
Francine Forrest was concerned, he was the one brick wall she could
not move. Without him she'd never find her kidnapped sister. But
could she avoid falling in love with him in the process?

#515 A WOMAN OF MYSTERY by Charlotte Douglas
A Memory Away...

More than muscles and a handsome face, Jordan Trouble was a
professional protector. And while the cop in him wanted to know
what caused a beautiful woman's amnesia, the man in him wanted to
know how she did what no other had—made him feel alive again.

#516 TO LANEY, WITH LOVE by Joyce Sullivan

A note from her supposedly dead husband sends Laney Dobson's
world into a tailspin. But the clues she and Ben Forbes follow lead
to the revelation of a lifetime of deceit—and unexpected passion in
Ben's arms.

Look us up on-line at: http://www.romance.net